A *Three on a Broomstick* Adventure

The Handwritten Book

by David Casler
acting on behalf of
Alec Pringle

Also by David Casler:

- The Story of the Great American Flying Broomstick
  Book 1: Genesis (on Kindle)
  *Dave discovers FOG and acquires "the power." He invents the
  flying broomstick and ends up in a heap of trouble.*

- The Story of the Great American Flying Broomstick
  Book 2: The Missing Wand (on Kindle)
  *Dave loses his duplicate wand. And the FAA hates broomsticks
  that fly. Some think it's all evil witchcraft.*

- The Story of the Great American Flying Broomstick
  Book 3: FOG at the Crossroads (on Kindle)
  *FOG loses the Holy Grail. The organization fractures as a result.
  Can Dave and Hardy put it all back together?*

- The Berki Blunder (on Kindle)
  The alien crew members of the Periwinkle *have come to earth to
  steal technology. Find out why USAF Colonel Wainwright thinks
  the English word for "Berki" is "blunder."*

- About Phillip (on Kindle)
  *Phillip is 15 and discovers he's a track star. Now if he can just
  deal with his father.*

See www.MtSneffelsPress.com for ordering information.

David Casler's Amazon author page can be found at
www.amazon.com/-/e/B0047I0Q4

A *Three on a Broomstick* Adventure

The Handwritten Book

by David Casler,
acting for Alec Pringle

Mt. Sneffels Press

Ridgway, Colorado

Mt. Sneffels Press
P.O. Box 98
Ridgway, CO 81432
U.S.A.

The book within a book within a book...

The books in my fantasy series, *The Story of the Great American Flying Broomstick,* make frequent reference to a series of books— and the resulting movies—called *Three on a Broomstick.*

The idea is that the hero of the *American Flying Broomstick* books is motivated and inspired by the eight young-adult books and movies in the *Three on a Broomstick* series. Its putative author, Alec Pringle, writes one of these books every year, detailing the adventures of John, Conan, and Alex, who possess a flying broomstick and use it for wondrous and magical adventures. The boys create their broomstick following instructions in a handwritten book given to them by an old fortune teller. And the *Three on a Broomstick* books are turned into movies by the fictional High Summit Motion Pictures firm. You can learn all about it in the *American Flying Broomstick* series.

The *Three on a Broomstick* series was not intended to exist in reality—it was only a literary device. That is...until now.

You are holding in your hands the first book in the *Three on a Broomstick* series, *The Handwritten Book.* Yes, there is a book within this book. And since *this* book is within the *American Flying Broomstick* series, the old, handwritten book is a book within a book within a book. And it's full of magic.

David Casler

To my mum.
Though no longer with us,
she inspires us still.

Three on a Broomstick
Book 1:
The Handwritten Book

by Alec Pringle

Chapter 1

When ten-year-old John Cunningham woke to the sound of his rusty alarm clock on the first Saturday in August, he had no idea that adventures lay ahead. The adventures would start that very day, but I won't whisper a word about them just yet, because it's not really fair that you should know about them before he does.

John rubbed his eyes, wondering why he was getting up so early on a Saturday. The sunlight streamed through the partially-closed blinds and caught him right in the face, making him squint. He lay back on his pillow and idly stroked the black and white cat that had jumped onto his chest. He couldn't think of any reason for being up. In fact, requiring John Cunningham to think when he first woke up was like trying to make chocolate milk out of mud—they may be the same color, but you certainly can't do it.

He pushed back the covers and swung his feet over the side, waiting to feel the chill of the hardwood floor. But, no! Before he'd even gotten his feet to the floor, they yelped! And not a little yelp either. In great surprise, he looked down at the floor to see what was so soft and squishy, and then in a flash he remembered why he had set the alarm.

There on the floor were his best mates, sleeping in their warm, squashy sleeping bags. Somehow in the night, Conan Tompkins had maneuvered himself so his head was waiting to meet John's feet. Conan, also ten years old—just the day before—was now twisting around to avoid John's other foot.

"Oh, sorry!" said John. "I didn't mean to do that."

Conan just wriggled further into his sleeping bag, pulling his pillow in with him. "Is it time to be up already? Can't be! What time is it?"

John glanced at his old alarm clock. The hour hand wiggled around a little bit depending on how you shook the clock, so he had to check it carefully. "It's seven o'clock. Dad says we need breakfast before we go to the Faire."

"Ohhhhhhh…" muttered Conan, slowly crawling to his feet in the chilly room. "Alex, wake up!"

Alex Baxter, who was also ten, was John's other best friend. In fact, the three were rarely separated. John's father, Fred Cunningham, and mother, Gertie, had promised to take the three of them to the Medieval Faire, but only if all three were up and dressed on time, since it was a bit of a drive from Manchester to Buxton. So John had suggested the sleepover.

Let's describe our three young heroes, now on the precipice of great adventure, because we have them all vertical and in a position where we can examine them more closely. John was the tallest by half a head. He had a round face—which he wished were a little thinner, like his dad's—blond hair rather closely cropped, and he was just a titch overweight, which he wished weren't the case, but that didn't stop him from eating what he pleased.

Conan didn't look anything like John. The most interesting feature about Conan was his ponytail. Now ponytails on boys are not that common, but Conan liked football—what Americans call 'soccer'—and played it every chance he got, and his favorite football player, who played for the home team, Manchester United, had a ponytail. And thus for the last four years, Conan absolutely refused to get a haircut, going so far as to bite the barber's hand, because he wanted his brown hair to look just like his hero's. So even though his two best friends often kidded him about it, Conan simply was going to have a ponytail and that was that!

And Alex? What do we say about Alex? Even though he really was ten, he was—oh, let's say it: small for his age. Add to that a bewildered, disheveled look, and you have a complete picture of Alex.

And Alex was the reason they were gathered this morning. Alex's favorite hobby was knights and armor. And castles. And fair maidens and swords and kings and queens.

The event slated for the day was a Medieval Faire, where tourists—and people like Alex—could go to watch jousting matches, see lots of people dressed in costume, eat medieval food, and generally get a good dose of things more properly belonging to King Arthur and the Round Table—although actually, truth be told, King Arthur lived before medieval times, but we won't tell Alex that just yet.

The boys dressed. John made his bed, at least he pulled the bedclothes up. His mum never quite approved of the way he made the bed and often came into the room to "make it the right way," with a strong hint he should do likewise, but he never did and she never pushed it. Meanwhile, Conan and Alex rolled up their sleeping bags. Conan had to help Alex with the knot on the string around the bag, because it kept springing loose, leaving Alex bewildered. When they were done, they piled the sleeping bags and pillows on John's bed, to be picked up later.

Breakfast was a happy affair. The Cunningham household was a happy one most of the time, although with three Cunningham children in the household, things were bound to get pesky here and there. John, Conan, and Alex sat at the giant round table in the middle of the Cunningham kitchen. Also in the kitchen were John's mum and dad. Now there are two more people I need to introduce: Katie and Miriam. Katie, whose mum always called her 'Catherine,' was 12 and very willing to boss John around, although, truth be told, John didn't listen to any of it. Katie was much taller than John and proud of telling everyone she was "almost a teenager." Sometimes Katie and her mum got into shouting matches, but they always made up, although sometimes this took a couple days. And this morning Katie seemed happy because she would have the house, and therefore the telly, to herself, so she was humming and helping Mum with the sausages.

Miriam was six. She had dark hair, much darker than anyone else in the family. And no, it wasn't dyed dark—it really was that dark. A very dark brown, but not quite black. She wore it in two braids, one above each ear. Sometimes she seemed morose, but today she was content because after breakfast she would spend the day with her best friend Janine, who lived across the street, which meant she wouldn't spend it with Katie, who bossed Miriam around.

Once John, Conan and Alex sat down, Alex began to talk. He talked lots, and he talked now. "They're going to do a jousting demonstration. I heard someone say that real jousting is too dangerous. Can you imagine that? I wish I could joust. I bet I would always win! You have to be very brave to try it, though."

"I'd bet!" interrupted Conan, a sausage speared on his fork and halfway to his mouth. "I'd make loads of money that way."

Conan wanted to bet on everything. One time when Conan wasn't around, John heard his mum and dad talking in the next room. "It's his father, that's why. He's got a gambling addiction. That's why they haven't any money. I've heard they're on the dole." John had no idea what the dole was, nor was he really certain what an addiction was. John wanted to defend Conan, but it was true that Conan wanted to bet on everything. And he almost always lost. John had stopped making bets with Conan, because when he did, Conan bet all the meager coins he had, and then he lost them to John and John didn't know how to give them back without making Conan feel even worse about losing his money in the first place.

"It's stupid to bet," said Miriam. "Anyway, Alex is too small to joust."

"I know that," said Alex sharply. "I just wish I could. When I grow up, I will."

"I don't think your mum would allow it," said Katie. She was right. Alex's mum didn't allow much. Ever since Alex's father died, she seemed to cling to her only son with particular ferocity. Alex didn't like this, but Mrs. Cunningham was always telling him to take care of his mum.

"Now, now, children," said Mum. She always said that when she sensed things getting out of hand. "Finish your hot chocolate, and we'll be off."

Chapter 2

The three boys were ready to leave. John's mother delivered Miriam safely across the street, and Katie settled herself in a chair in front of the telly set and put in a *Harry Potter* DVD. Dad had trouble getting the front door open after Mum returned—the door always jammed—but once it was open they headed out. Conan and Alex jumped through the front door at the same time, and the interesting thing is that they fit, since Alex was so small. John followed behind.

The Cunninghams lived on Brixton Street in Wythenshawe, a section of Manchester in the northwestern part of England. The street was not very pretty—a collection of mostly run-down homes built nearly a century before when there were big woolen mills in the area. They lived here because both Fred and Gertie Cunningham worked close by—John's father was an accountant for Beckwith & Howe, the big financial firm, and John's mother was a computer programmer for Goodin's Software, which made accounting software used by companies such as Beckwith & Howe.

John overheard them one day when he switched off the telly and they were in the kitchen and didn't realize the telly wasn't making noise anymore. Mother wanted to move further out of town, because she didn't like the area, plus she wanted a bigger garden, but Dad gently reminded her that John's best friends lived right next door, plus moving further out of town meant a longer commute for both—as it was, they could walk three short blocks to a Metrolink station—and therefore less time with their three children. And so they agreed to stay here.

John had felt guilty about it ever since—it seemed as though they were living in a place where they didn't want to just because of him. He often wondered what life would be like without Conan and Alex, but couldn't imagine it. Sometimes he felt torn by his loyalty to his parents and his loyalty to his friends. He tried telling Conan about it one day, but Conan was unhappy because of one of his father's long, unexplained absences, and told John he should be happy he had both parents. John didn't bring it up again.

Dad climbed into the ten-year-old Jaguar saloon he'd bought from a former boss. Mum took the passenger seat. John sat in his usual position, right behind his father. To his left, against the window, sat Conan, and Alex was in the same spot he was always in when the three went together—in the middle.

"Why do I always get the middle?" he complained.

"Because you fit there best," said Conan.

Alex grumbled and looked discontented, but otherwise said nothing. The contrast between the two boys could not be more complete—Conan was athletic and loved football more than anything else; whereas, Alex was bookish and hated any kind of physical exertion.

John enjoyed trips to the country, probably because his parents took him there so rarely. Instead of houses on top of each other, they were more spread out, each in its own garden. The Cunninghams had a little garden in front of their home in Whythenshawe, and another one in back, to be sure, but Mum's promised flowers never seemed to bloom and Dad took to hiring out the grass cutting. John secretly wished for the fantastic gardens he saw at the zoo or at the big manor houses, but realized more garden meant more chores for him. As it was, he was barely big enough to push Dad's hand-push mower, and if the grass got too high, he simply got stuck. But he was old enough to trim the hedges, not necessarily a chore he enjoyed because he always stuck himself on the cut-off hedge limbs. And he still remembered the time when he was seven, when he fell backwards into the rose bush and Conan had to rescue him. It left him with scars all over his arms and face, most of which were gone by now, except one on his inner arm that was about an inch long. Mum said she couldn't see it, but he knew it was there. He'd never liked roses since and always complained when Mum put on rose-scented perfume.

The fivesome picked their way through the streets of Wythenshawe, finding streets that were bigger and bigger until they turned onto the high street that led them to the motorway.

6

John knew it wasn't a good idea to make too much noise in the back seat when his father was driving, so he didn't respond much to Alex's constant stream of explanations of knights in shining armor. Sometimes John thought Alex was born in the wrong century. And, anyway, he had heard somewhere that people were actually smaller a few centuries ago, so maybe Alex would've fit in better back then.

In short order they were driving on the high street again, since the motorway didn't go very far in the direction of the Faire. John watched the street signs carefully, since he intended to be old enough to drive someday. They traveled along A523, then made a left hand turn onto A537. By this time they were in woods, so different from Wythenshawe!

Conan became animated when they went by a schoolyard where the football field backed onto the high road. "Lousy kick," he commented, pointing to the goalie in blue shorts. "Even I could do better than that!" John never knew whether to agree or not—after all, Conan was the football expert.

Alex was still in full flower about knights. He described all the pieces of armor a knight wore—from the helm and gauntlets to the breastplate and greaves. This didn't mean anything to John, so Alex proceeded to explain what each was used for and how it was made. For about the hundredth time. Alex was remarkably persistent and patient, acting as though John were genuinely interested, which John tried to be.

The Medieval Faire was set up in a meadow near a wood, not far from Buxton, a very pretty town by and large, if you ignored the filling stations and the supermarket. Except for right downtown, where there are still houses with thatched roofs, each home had a garden, and many were very lovely, John thought. He wasn't pleased with the one that had so many roses, however. He unconsciously rubbed the scar on his inner arm.

Dad drove the old Jaguar over the bumpy field to park it where the attendants were giving directions. "They always want us to park so close together," he grumbled. "Don't know how we'll ever get out." And, sure enough, another car parked right next to theirs before they could open the doors.

John squeezed out and joined Conan and Alex in trailing along behind Mum and Dad. Dad flinched at the entry fee—£5 per adult and £3 each for John, Conan and Alex—but a promise was a promise and there was no turning back now.

They squinted at the programs the gate attendant gave them.

10:00 a.m. Jousting exhibition, Main Arena

11:00 a.m. Trebuchet competition, Round One, Main Arena

12:00 noon Lunch serving in Main Tent, £4/person, £2.50/child under 12

1:00 p.m. Chess tournament begins, Tent 2

2:00 p.m. Jousting exhibition Main Arena, also Blacksmithing exhibition, Tent 5

3:00 p.m. Trebuchet competition, Round Two, Main Arena

4:00 p.m. Jousting match, Main Arena

5:00 p.m. Trebuchet competition, Finals, Main Arena

6:00 p.m. Costume judging, Tent 4

All day Commercial Booths (see Page 5 for list and Page 6 for map)

"We can't stay all day," warned Dad, to Alex's disappointment "I promised we'd have you home by six." But he hastened to add, "We can still see most of the Faire."

Since it was nearly ten o'clock, they hurried in the direction of the Main Arena, with Alex taking the lead and rushing along with surprising speed given his short stature. John lost sight of him several times, but Conan ran ahead to grab Alex and slow him down. Alex was so eager to get there he pushed his way through the crowd, nearly upsetting an old lady's fizzy drink, which made her rebuke him angrily. Dad said "sorry," and pointed Alex in the right direction.

The Faire was a visual delight for the three boys. Medieval times must've been very colorful, because about a third of the faire-goers wore costumes of some sort—here and there a jouster, some people in various leather garb intending to represent knights, with some in chain mail and others in plate armor, and many of the women in long, colorful dresses. The favorite color seemed to be green.

Mum and Dad went to sit at the top of the arena, but John, Conan and Alex were small enough that they slipped to the very

8

front, up by the rail. The horses were so big! The announcer's voice was hard to understand, but it sounded as though he was telling people about each of the jousters who came onto the field.

There were four. One, dressed in shiny armor that John thought might really be aluminum instead of steel, was atop a mighty steed that was mostly white but had tiny black flecks all over. The next wore dark gray armor with a pointed helmet that sported a long red feather. He had a black horse—a bigger horse than John had ever seen. The third had black-painted armor, presumably to make himself harder to see, although John could see him very well indeed. His horse was equally large and brown. The fourth wore dark gray armor with a coat of arms painted on the front and back.

Each of the jousters, all dressed as knights, had long jousting sticks called lances. From where John stood, they looked heavy and hard to balance. The horses seemed ready to go, because they were pawing the ground and generally not behaving themselves.

A long rope stretched sideways across the field. The announcer said something more, and knights one and two lined up, one at each end of the field on opposite sides of the rope. Soon they were galloping toward each other, lances held at the ready, but to Alex's disappointment, they passed each other, lances intact.

"…no contact is permitted in modern exhibitions, of course…" said the announcer, although the rest was hard to make out.

The horsemen charged each other again and again, with different knights taking turns. The crowd yelled with each race, and once one of the knights dropped his lance, which John thought must have been terribly embarrassing.

"This is so cool!" shouted Alex.

"Why don't they do anything?" asked Conan.

"Let's go look at the booths," suggested John.

But Alex was not to be moved. It was nearly 10:30 a.m. when the exhibition was finally over, and only then would Alex budge.

"I'm hungry," he said. "Let's see if we can find something cool to eat."

And so they waited for John's parents to collect them. They could see people on the field moving the trebuchets into position, which Alex wanted to watch. John's dad thought it was too early to get something to eat. "It'll spoil your appetite," he said. "We'll come back for the catapults later."

"Trebuchets," corrected Alex.

Following the crowd, they worked their way out of the arena toward the booths. Different vendors were in costumes of various colors, mostly green and yellow, although here and there one could see a brownish red. Apparently really strong colors didn't exist in medieval times, to hear Alex explain it.

They looked in various booths, some of which had wares that appeared suspiciously modern. One sold jewelry, another cloth, still another cotton candy. "Yuck," said Alex. "They didn't have anything like that back then!"

The smells coming from the booths were alternately wonderful and awful. The wonderful smells came from the food vendors, some offering bits of pheasant on a stick, others soup, some candy. Some of the awful smells came from the candle booths. Some of the candles were in boxes, just like John had seen at the shopping mall, but in one booth they were making candles by dipping strings in hot wax. The perfumes they were adding to the wax made John's nose wrinkle.

"Are you using beeswax?" asked Alex. He was assured that they had beeswax candles, but most were made of tallow, a waxy substance made from animal fat. The lady making candles even let Alex dip a couple candles, which made him grin from ear to ear. "Just like they used to do in castles," he confided to John on their way out. Mum said she liked the various candles and would shop here for awhile.

At last Dad and the boys came to a small tent with a simple sign outside: "Fortunes Told, Guaranteed Accurate, £1 (children 50p)." The sign looked as though it had been used many, many times. It was propped up on an old folding chair.

"How can they be guaranteed accurate?" said Conan. "I'll bet they're not!"

"They're probably so vague that no one can tell," said Dad, clearly not impressed.

10

"Let's do it!" said Alex. "Just for fun!"

But the problem was simple. Dad wasn't going to pay for it. Finally, Alex ponied up 25p, Conan had 30p, and John had 45p. That was only £1 total. They were 50p short.

John considered. Alex really wanted to do this. Conan looked like he could go either way. "Maybe she can do the three of us at once for a quid," he said. "Let's ask."

So, without waiting for permission, they pushed aside the tent flap and stepped inside.

The tent wasn't large, perhaps eight feet square, and since it was a fairly warm, sunny day, it was stifling hot inside. In the middle was a table about four feet long. An old-fashioned steamer trunk lay at the back of the tent, its lid closed. And just inside the tent were three folding chairs for people to use while waiting to have their fortunes told.

Behind the table sat an elderly lady who had more wrinkles than John had ever seen, even on his Aunt Emma, and she was older than Manchester itself. The old lady had a scarf wrapped around her head, many beads around her neck, and wore a flowing dress and a shawl, even though it was hot inside the tent. John thought she must be sweating to death. He figured someone that old should be wearing glasses—his Aunt Emma was forever looking for her glasses—but the old lady had none.

On the table sat an ancient wooden box, just big enough to be a cash box. And in the middle of the table was a crystal ball, about five inches in diameter, perched on an intricate metal base with lots of carvings and iron lacework. And to one side was an old kerosene lantern, which John guessed was there so the old woman could see its reflections in the crystal ball. He wondered why she needed it, since there was plenty of light coming through the tent walls and through the openings in the sides of the tent.

Sitting in a corner was a sour old man, whose face was as lined as that of the old woman's. John instinctively didn't like him, and his presence made the three of them nervous.

The old woman was telling the fortune of a woman who was dressed in a green pant suit with a white blouse. She smelled faintly like roses. John crinkled his nose and looked at Alex. The three of them sat on the waiting chairs, very quietly, lest they

11

disturb the old woman. She alternately looked at the woman's palm and into the crystal ball.

"You are in business, I see. Perhaps you are a shop owner?" she said.

"Yes," said the woman. "I have a tea shop in Bristol."

"Business could be better, I see. You are worried about one of your employees. A young lady with dark hair."

"Yes. How did you know?"

"I can see her. I think she cheats you. You would do well to watch her. But you also have another employee, a young man with a ponytail."

Conan shrunk lower in his seat and held his hand over his hair.

"Yes, that's true, too. I've never been quite sure what to think of him."

"He's reliable. You are correct to trust him. Now, you are thinking of offering a new menu. I encourage you to do that. It will be very successful."

"How did you know?"

"Oh, I can see it. Yes, it will bring in new customers. Well, I think that will do," said the old lady.

The tourist, obviously rattled by such a specific reading, rose from her chair and left without even saying goodbye.

"Now my dears," said the old lady to the three. The old man stirred in the back without saying anything.

John's hair rose on the back of his neck. He was the first to speak.

"Uh, we don't have enough money for all three of us, so we were wondering if you could…uh…do all three of us together for a quid?" He stammered, wondering how they'd gotten in the tent. For some reason it seemed very quiet, not at all like the hubbub they'd left outside. He wished Dad would step inside.

She smiled, but the old man shook his head. "Of course, dearies," she said. "Why don't you pull up two more chairs, so you can all sit here at once."

"The price is fifty pence each," growled the old man.

"Marco, they're children. I'll do it and won't hear a word to the contrary!"

The old man called Marco didn't look happy. He settled back in his chair to scowl at John, Conan and Alex. Alex took the chair already in place and left John and Conan to grab two chairs.

"Now let me see your palms, my dears," she said in her creepy voice.

Tentatively, they put their right hands on the table next to the crystal ball, palms up. Conan, on the left, couldn't quite reach, so he put his hand to the other side of the crystal ball.

"Interesting. Very interesting!" said the old lady. "I don't think I've ever seen anything quite so interesting," she said.

"Uh, interesting in what way?" queried John.

"I think each of you has magic in your blood. Have you ever tried any magic?" she asked, her eyes boring into John's.

"No," squeaked John. "We don't know any magic tricks." Beside him, Alex shivered.

"Let me see what's in the crystal ball," she said in a dreamy voice. She pulled her shawl closer as though cold and edged forward on her seat. "You can put your hands away, dears." All three boys withdrew their arms in an instant. The old woman gazed into the crystal ball, finally taking it in her hands and lifting it up, holding it between her eyes and the lantern. At last, she smiled.

"I knew today would be the day. That's why I brought it."

"Brought what?" asked Conan, who seemed the most skeptical.

But at this point John thought he would believe anything. After all, she'd told the tourist's fortune in a way that seemed very real.

"I see you three riding a broomstick!"

"A broomstick!" exclaimed Conan. "You mean like witches?"

"Exactly, my dear. A broomstick. All three of you," she said, "on one extra-long broomstick."

"How are we supposed to do that?" asked John, now as skeptical as Conan. "I mean, you see that in the movies, but not in real life! How do we ride a broomstick?"

The old man called Marco got up to hover behind the old woman. "Can you be sure? Not these children. You shouldn't tell them such things!"

"I will tell them what I see," she said firmly. "Sit down."

The old man hesitated, then finally did what he was told.

She went on. "I see the three of you riding a broomstick. But first you must build one. It's a complex process. Are you up to making a broomstick? It is, after all, foretold. And my crystal ball is never wrong."

"We can make anything," piped up Alex. John wasn't so sure.

"Well then, it's settled. Since it is foretold, I will give you the book. But you must promise me to give the book to no one else, and to be very, very careful with it. It contains many secrets of magic. You must…"

"NO!" shouted the old man. "You can't give it away!" He jumped to his feet.

"Sit down and shut up," she insisted, turning in her chair to face Marco. "These boys are to have it, and no one else!" Marco was quiet but did not sit down. The old woman turned to the boys. "Now you be very careful with it."

"Can we show it to our parents?" asked John, thinking in practical terms for the first time since entering the tent.

"Of course," she smiled. She pushed back her chair and with effort drew herself erect. Her beads jangled. She turned to the ragged, old trunk, held together with long leather belts, and struggled with the latch. It fell away with a clunk. She stooped and pulled up the lid.

Dad stuck his head into the tent. "Who's shouting?" he asked. "Are you boys all right?"

John piped up first. "We're fine. We're almost done. She's going to give us a book."

"Are you crazy?" shouted Marco. He put his hand down to close the trunk's lid.

"Get out of my way, you stupid old man!" insisted the fortune teller. "The boys are to have the book! Not you!"

"But it should be mine!" insisted Marco.

Dad cleared his throat. "Perhaps it would be better if we left," he suggested.

Conan turned around, but John held onto him. "What is the book?" John asked, as politely as he could, since his father was standing right behind him.

"What book?" asked Dad, confused.

"I don't know," said John. "She said she was giving us a book about how to build a flying broomstick."

Dad shook his head. "I think we'd better leave."

"Wait!" commanded the old woman. She pushed the old man back, who collapsed in his chair looking very cross. In a moment, she flung back the lid of the trunk. John craned to see what was inside, but it looked mostly like junk. She rummaged in a corner and in a moment fished out an oversize diary, complete with a latch and a lock. She thrust the book at John.

"You are the leader, I see. You will find everything you need to know inside here. Okay, boys, I want all of you to touch my palm. Just put your index fingers there. Not so hard, Conan."

"How did you know my name?" asked Conan. But he didn't push as hard.

Once the boys were all touching her palm, she spoke again. "I give you magic."

Instantly the boys felt a shiver that went from their heads to their feet.

"What was that?" said Conan, pulling his finger away and rubbing it.

"What did you do to the boys?" asked Dad, sounding wary.

"They'll learn as they read the book. Now I must get back to work."

Marco jumped up. "No!"

"Be quiet, you silly old man. And sit back down. We have more customers. Young man, you owe me one quid. That's what we agreed to."

"Oh," said John, who had forgotten about paying. He stuck the heavy book under his left arm and fished in his pocket. He pulled out his coins. "C'mon, Conan and Alex. You too."

Conan and Alex fished in their pockets.

"Eighty pence, ninety, ninety-five. Where's the other five pence?" John looked first at Conan and then at Alex.

Alex dropped to his hands and knees and looked around. "Maybe I dropped it."

"Here," said Dad. He pulled out a pocketful of coins, selected a £1 coin, and handed it to the old lady. "We'd better be going."

He held back the tent flap and whisked the boys out, glad the business was done. The old man sat in his chair, looking unhappy indeed. The old lady was back behind her table, holding the crystal ball in her hands between her and the lamp. She didn't look happy, either. She glanced at John. John shivered when their eyes met.

Chapter 3

Grateful they'd kept their own pocket change, the boys broke into an immediate babble as they walked along the crowded, noisy concourse between the booths and tents.

"What's in the book?" Alex asked, grabbing for it.

"Yes, indeed, boys. What happened in there?" asked Dad. By this time they had joined Mum, who had been at the candle booth all this time and now had a heavy shopping bag.

John told him, with Conan and Alex chiming in with the details. "And so she said we were supposed to have this book. She said it was foretold. Then the old man got really angry. I don't like him."

"Let me see the book," said Dad in that tone of voice that said he wasn't happy either. John handed it to him. The book was fairly large for a diary, perhaps the size of the notebook paper you use in school, and about an inch thick. It had a brown leather cover with some sort of fancy design embossed. And it looked like it had been used, because here and there the shiny leather surface had been rubbed so it wasn't shiny anymore. The pages looked dirty along the edges for three-quarters of an inch; the rest seemed unused.

But there was a problem.

There was a clasp that went from the back cover into a latch on the front cover. And it wouldn't open.

"Maybe we should take this back," suggested Dad.

"No!" yelled Alex. "It's full of magic!"

"I don't think so, in this day and age. Tell me again why she gave it to you?"

"She said it would tell us how to make a flying broomstick. I bet it doesn't," said Conan. "Here, I bet 25 pence it doesn't."

"Then why did the old man want it so badly?" asked John. "Conan, Alex, and I want to keep it, right?" The other two boys nodded their heads vigorously.

Dad looked dubious, but handed the book back to John. The three boys crowded around.

"We need the key," said Alex. "How are we going to find out what's inside?"

"Don't know," said Conan. "Maybe we can pick the lock? My father's good at picking locks." He paused. "Well, he is when he's around."

Mum took the old book from John. "Aunt Emma has a diary like this. Maybe she'll have a key that fits."

"Mr. Cunningham," said Conan, tugging on John's dad's sleeve. "I think that old man named Marco is following us. Look. Over there."

They all swiveled to look in the direction Conan pointed. Sure enough, Marco stood about fifty feet away through the crowd, now looking at a booth that sold cotton candy. He glanced furtively at the three boys, then went back to studying the cotton candy. He wasn't buying any, however.

"Maybe we should just take this book back right now," said Mum.

"No!" chorused the trio. "She wanted us to have it!"

"I'm hungry," added Alex.

Chapter 4

The two adults and three boys sat under a circus-sized canopy, listening to the rain now dripping on the canvas from the gathering storm, savoring the smell of sizzling meats. They'd been tempted by roast lamb, roast beef, roast ham, roast chicken, roast goose, roast pheasant, and other things they weren't sure of, all roasting. They'd made their choices (the boys wished for hamburgers, but there was nothing that looked like it should go between a bun), settling for roasted Cornish game hens.

"In the castles, they used to just eat with their fingers," said Alex to no one.

"I think I'd prefer a fork," said Mum. "Have you seen any?"

"I like these spices," commented Dad.

17

"They didn't have many spices in the time of the castles," replied Alex. "I think they've got too many spices on this to be real castle food."

"There's Marco," said Conan. "See, he just came into the tent."

Sure enough, he had. He'd put on a coat because of the chilly drizzle, but it was the same old man. John thought he looked downright evil in black leather. He had gray-white hair, slicked straight back, and it needed cutting because it sort of straggled past the collar of his jacket. Marco's eyes were darting all over the crowd. For a moment, John's eyes met Marco's, and then Marco started working his way down the tables, elbowing his way past the many tourists and making a man spill his drink. He muttered an apology and hurried on, leaving the man spluttering something about buying him another.

"Who has the book?" John asked.

"I do. It's in my lap," said Alex.

"Quick! Hide it!"

"Where?"

John thought for a moment. Alex sat across the table from him, and soon Marco would be upon them.

"Sit on it!" said John.

Alex made the transfer just as Marco came up behind John. Marco addressed himself to Dad.

"I'm so sorry to trouble you, sir, but my wife made a mistake. I am looking for her diary. She accidentally gave it to your son."

"It wasn't an accident!" chimed John and Conan at the same time.

"I don't understand," said Dad. "I was there. I think she truly intended it for these boys."

Marco's face was anxious. "Perhaps I could purchase it from you? Maybe ten pounds?" He pulled out a worn leather wallet and started leafing inside, counting out greasy £1 notes.

Dad vacillated. "What do you think, boys?"

"Why do you want it?" asked John, as politely as he could because Mum and Dad were sitting next to them.

"Ah," said Marco, obviously trying to think up an excuse. "It's an old family heirloom. A very important book. It has a sort of…

18

well…magic of its own…uh, it would be such a shame to have it leave the family. Twenty pounds?"

"Not a chance," said John.

"No way," said Alex.

"We're keeping it," said Conan. "The old woman said we were to have it. She says it was foretold."

Marco's eyes were darting over the boys and fastened on Mum's shopping bag. His hand inched toward it. "Ah, well. She's been known to make mistakes," he muttered.

"Her fortunes are guaranteed," piped up Conan. "Says so right on her sign. And she said it would tell us how to make a flying broomstick!"

Marco cringed. "Not so loud! Thirty pounds. Please—It's all I have." He held up the dirty notes so they could all look.

"So it really will!" said Conan. "You were right, John. I owe you 25 pence."

"No you don't," replied John. "I never took your bet."

"Mr. Marco," said Dad loudly. "It appears the boys' minds are made up. If they decide differently, we know where your tent is."

Marco looked at them for a long moment, fear and pleading in his eyes. Looking like an overage prize fighter who had been badly beaten in the ring, he turned slowly and walked back to the entrance to the tent. He seemed wilted.

But he did not leave the tent, pretending to interest himself in the roast goose display. He didn't buy any, and occasionally glanced at the boys.

"That man gives me the creeps," said Alex.

Chapter 5

I would tell you all about the rest of their day at the Faire, but since your mind is now on the book with the leather clasp, let's concentrate on that. Needless to say, John's, Conan's, and Alex's minds were on the book, too. And on Marco, who seemed to be watching them from a distance. One time Dad set after him, but he promptly disappeared. Mum suggested Dad find a policeman and report Marco's stalking, but not only did Marco seem to disappear whenever they went after him, they never saw a policeman the entire afternoon. And it was drizzling constantly now that the storm had arrived, so after watching the trebuchet competition and one last jousting demonstration, the boys were only too grateful to be heading toward the car where it was warm and dry.

Conan always seemed to be the first to see Marco. He spotted him as they were getting into the car.

"He's writing something down," he reported.

"I can't see," said Alex, twisting around in the back seat. "I can never see from the middle seat!"

Dad stopped the car and got out to look, but Marco had disappeared. He got back into the car. "Why do you boys want to keep the book so badly, anyway? You could've made thirty quid. That's ten quid each!"

"The old woman said we were supposed to have it," said John, peering out the window at the receding fairgrounds. "Do you think he's following us?"

"She said it will tell us how to make a flying broomstick," said Conan, twisting around to see where John was looking.

"I'll bet it's full of magic," said Alex. "Can I see it?" John handed the book to Alex. Alex fiddled with the catch on the latch, but no amount of poking or prodding was going to open it. Next, Alex pulled the cover back.

"Don't ruin the book!" exclaimed John, grabbing at it.

Alex pulled it away. "I'm just trying to peek inside. See? I can pull it back about a half inch. Look! This isn't a normal book. It's full of handwriting!"

John took the book and did the same thing Alex did. He could only see a tiny corner of each page. But it was true—every page was handwritten, as far toward the center of the book as he could see. The pages toward the back of the book seemed to be blank. He handed the book to Conan across Alex.

"Really tiny writing," commented Conan. "Maybe we can cut the strap when we get home."

"Good idea," said John.

Meanwhile Alex was peering out the back of the car through the mist. "I don't think Marco is following us," he said. "Nobody's behind us at all."

"Good riddance," said Mum.

Chapter 6

It was raining hard when they came to a stop in front of the Cunningham home. Dad got out first to unlock the door to the house, since there was no stoop and everyone would get wet if they waited as he struggled with the key. The door had been the bane of their existence for as long as John could remember. He was five years old when his parents bought the house, and the door wouldn't open for the estate agent when she showed them around. And then when they moved in, it took Dad a solid fifteen minutes to unlock the door. They had had the locksmith around to look at it, but of course it opened perfectly for him, so other than make them an extra key, he did nothing. John had his own key, since sometimes he came home from day care before his parents were home, especially when the Metrolink was extra-crowded. And day care ended promptly at 6:00 p.m., so John would sometimes pretend he saw his parents waiting outside, and would run the three blocks to his home and let himself in. If the door worked, that is. The last two times he'd come home early, he couldn't get the door to open, so he went go over to Alex's house to warm up until he saw the lights on in his own home.

When Dad finally got the door open, John ran toward the house with the handwritten book under his shirt. He didn't know quite why, but felt he should protect it from the elements. Conan beat him to the door, but Alex straggled behind.

"Now wait for your mum," said Dad, admonishing them all, even though she wasn't Conan's or Alex's mum.

The three boys ran to the dinner table and plopped down the book. Meanwhile, Dad turned on lights and helped Mum with her coat. With some reluctance, he closed the door tight, since sometimes the door was hard to open from the inside as well.

"Can you cut the strap?" bubbled John.

"Dear," said Mum. "Let's get something to eat first. And Conan and Alex need to ring their parents to let them know we're home."

"No!" said Conan. "Let's cut the strap!"

"Call home first!" insisted Mum.

So first Conan and then Alex called their parents. Alex's mum wanted him to come home right away, but Alex said "in a minute."

Mum got out her big shears, the ones she used to cut leather for her crafts. The boys crowded around eagerly. Mum tried to cut the strap, but it seemed too strong.

"There isn't even a dent," remarked Mum, trying again harder. They all peered round to look. Each of the boys took a turn, but the strap would not give way.

"We need something stronger," said Conan.

"I'll bet the book is magic," said Alex, jumping up and down. "It'll be impossible to cut."

Dad spoke up. "Let me try. I've got a box cutter. Very sharp. Stand back now—I don't want any accidents." Dad took the book and looked it over. "You're right—you can't see where the shears touched it." He put the book on the table and used his sharp box cutter. "That's odd," he said. "It's like the knife just slides over it. Let me try my big screwdriver on the lock."

"The book is magic," repeated Alex.

"Can't be. There's no such thing as real magic," said Conan. "I'll bet 25 pence Mr. Cunningham gets it open with his big screwdriver."

"No," said John. "Don't bet."

"All right!" said Alex, sure his money was safe.

As it turned out, Alex was quite right. Dad had a very big screwdriver indeed, and tried poking, turning, prodding, prying and generally all he could think of to do, but he could not bust the latch nor could he make it come open. And the most amazing thing was that nothing he did left the slightest mark on the book. Not even a scratch. Even when the screwdriver got loose from him and both screwdriver and book went flying onto the floor.

"Sorry, Conan," said Dad. "I can't make it do anything. Not anything at all."

Conan put his hand into his pocket and pulled out two 10p pieces and one 5p piece and pushed them across the table to Alex, who pocketed them eagerly.

"You shouldn't take Conan up on his bets," said John. "He always loses. Mum, didn't you say Aunt Emma has a diary just like this one? Do you think her key will fit this lock?"

"It's possible, dear. But every key is different."

"Can you ask her?"

"Perhaps we can have her for tea sometime," suggested Dad, eyeing his screwdriver for straightness. "I think I bent it. I don't see how I could have done."

"Tomorrow?" asked Alex. Actually, he almost shouted because he was so eager. "I can come too," he said, neatly inviting himself. "And Conan!"

"She lives in Leeds, Alex. I don't know what her schedule is."

"There's not a single mark on this book," mused Dad.

"That's because it's magic!" said Alex, very confidently, as though he dealt with magic every day and knew all about it.

Chapter 7

Well, as it turned out, the earliest Aunt Emma could come was two weeks hence, which made it the third Saturday in August. Actually, Aunt Emma was Mum's aunt, which made her John's great aunt. John was her favorite grand nephew (although John thought the reason for this was because he was her only grand nephew) and she always brought him sweets. She was quite flattered by the thought that her key might unlock something interesting to John, so much so that she brought her own diary.

And, as it turned out, her diary was identical to the old handwritten book, though it seemed newer and better cared for. There were no worn spots and the edges of the pages were gilded and clean. Aunt Emma took great pleasure in showing John, Conan, and Alex how the diary was locked and unlocked. Interestingly, though, she would not open her book for the three boys, though they begged her to do so. She said too many secrets from her life were written in there, even something she wrote when John was born. "I only write important things in here," she said mysteriously.

And also, very interestingly, it seemed that her key fit the lock on the old handwritten book. Her key was on a jangly key ring that was really a collection of several key rings all linked together.

23

And some of the things on the various key rings were not keys at all, but rather funny little metal ornaments. But she knew just which key fit her diary, and she tried it in the old handwritten book. "It feels just like it does when I turn the key in my own diary," she said, very confidently pressing on the latch. "But now that's funny. I can't make it come open, see now, it should open just the way mine does. I'm quite certain the key fits."

"You could feel it turning?" asked John, very concerned.

"Oh, yes! I'm sure I turned it the right way. I can feel the mechanism. It should be open now. See how the lever presses in, just like this." She showed John, Conan and Alex, who were all gathered around. "When I do this on mine, the catch springs back. Perhaps it needs a spot of oiling."

Dad had a small can of oil that he used for oiling door hinges. He fetched the can while John carried the book to the kitchen counter, away from the couch where his very puzzled Aunt sat stroking the black and white cat. Dad put a single drop into the key mechanism and John worked it back and forth, but the latch would not come loose.

"How are we supposed to build a broomstick if we can't open the book?" complained Conan.

"What's this?" asked Aunt Emma, who by now was standing to watch, her hand on John's shoulder.

"The old lady who told our fortune. She gave us the book," said Alex. "She said it had instructions in it to make a flying broomstick!"

Aunt Emma smiled her maternal smile. "Yes, of course, Alex," she said in a voice that gave away the fact that she didn't believe a word of it.

"Honey," said Mum, speaking to John. He wished she wouldn't call him that in front of Conan and Alex. "Please put the book away. It's time for tea."

Conan and Alex followed John to his room, the three of them trundling down the narrow hallway. The walls were crowded with family pictures.

"Why won't the book open?" hissed Conan, whispering as though John's bed might overhear them accidentally.

"I tell you, it's because the book is magic!" insisted Alex. "We need to use magic to open it."

"So we just say 'abracadabra' or something like that?" whispered Conan doubtfully.

"I don't know," said Alex, staring at the ceiling as though the answer were written there.

Chapter 8

For two whole weeks, John, Conan and Alex would gather every day to look at the handwritten book. But I'll admit, every day they looked at it a little less. After all, it was the last two weeks of summer break. Conan kept dragging them to the football pitch, but Alex was no good at kicking a ball, so John would throw the ball and Conan would play goalie. Sometimes John would be goalie, but Conan could always kick the ball past him. Even when both John and Alex played goalie together, Conan would get the ball into the net two times out of three, and it didn't seem fun at such odds.

Conan was a member of a local football team, so twice a week John and Alex would watch him play. And on alternate days there were practices, too, but Alex didn't always go to watch, thinking the practices were boring. Sometimes Alex went to the local library to look up books on magic, but all they told him how to do was turn a rabbit into a hat and things like that. Alex didn't think that would be useful in the case of the handwritten book.

The summer afternoons were warm, the grass was green on the path by the river, and sometimes the boys would just wander for hours. One time they got lost and had to ask directions from a policeman, who chided them for being so far from home. It was nearly six o'clock, so the policeman paid for a call at a phone booth so John could call his dad, who came to pick them up in the old Jaguar. Dad was not particularly happy, seeing as it was rush hour and very crowded, but John thought he looked relieved. The three boys did not say anything on the way home, and Conan and Alex went to their respective houses with only a perfunctory good-bye. Dad followed John to his room and gave him a good talking-to. John protested that if he had his own mobile phone he could call home, but that didn't get him anywhere. Embarrassed, John spent a few minutes with the handwritten book and then went to watch the telly.

Chapter 9

Finally, on the first Monday of September, it was time for school to start.

The boys would be in their sixth and final year at Allerton Primary School, only three blocks from their home. And, as they had for the last several years, John, Conan and Alex were expected to walk to school, rain or shine. They had to cross the High Street in front of the school, but there was a signal and even a crossing guard. None of them felt they needed the crossing guard now that their years were in the double digits, but they had no choice.

Allerton Primary School consisted of a collection of three very different buildings. The Old Hall, as it was called, was nearly 100 years old with high ceilings and archways for the doors. It wasn't very big, but it had a ground floor and a first floor, and it was rumored there was a basement through a door that was always locked. The school staff said that's where the furnace was, but no student was ever permitted in the basement, and the stories that circulated were enough to make anyone's hair stand on end, especially if a pupil disappeared for any length of time. The pupils usually came back and claimed they were sick, but sometimes pupils disappeared without a trace, and even though the staff said the pupils had moved, the other pupils gave each other knowing looks and sat a little straighter in class. The school custodian was very old and very fierce-looking—not the sort of person a child asked questions of. He did his work in silence.

The rest of the school had been destroyed during a bombing in World War II. Residents think it was a stray bomb intended for the factory only a quarter mile away—a factory that had now been converted into large condominium flats for those who didn't want to live in the suburbs. And so New Hall had been built, but New Hall was only one story high and sort of rambling, with twenty classrooms and a cafeteria. New Hall was called "utilitarian" by people who paid attention to what it looked like, which did not include John and Conan, but Alex always said Old

Hall looked more like a castle and New Hall more like a factory. New Hall had high ceilings and big windows to let in the light, which was admittedly weak during the winter months.

There was one more building, not very big, which housed an art classroom and an auditorium where the choir would practice. This was built after New Hall, and since people didn't want to call it the Really New Hall or the Newest Hall, they picked Sudbury Hall. No one seemed to remember why, but rumor was that the head teacher at the time named it after himself, but no one could prove it.

John, Conan and Alex lined up with the rest of the sixth-years in the courtyard in front of Old Hall, everyone looking the same in their pale blue shirts, navy trousers, black shoes and ties that were mostly navy except for the red stripes. Since it was a hot day, they didn't wear their light blue school sweaters. Alex's pants were a little too short. When the bell rang, they followed others down to their first class. They had most of their classes together, except choir, which Conan resolutely refused to join, and their physical education class, in which John and Conan did competitive sports and Alex would be doing cooperative sports, at least for the first three months.

They met at lunch in the cafeteria in New Hall to compare notes.

"They've given us too much homework already," said John, crunching a carrot.

"We're not even studying the Middle Ages," complained Alex. "We have to study government, whatever that is."

"They don't have football team trials for a week," muttered Conan, opening the sack lunch he'd brought from home and peering inside. "I wish I could buy a lunch. My sandwich is always gooey."

Their favorite teacher, by mutual consent, was Mr. Hume. Jack Hume was one of those people whose age you couldn't really tell. He always wore the same white shirt and always—always—wore the school tie—the only faculty member to do so. Sometimes students teased him, wondering if he only had one and wore it every day, but he always said he had exactly two, though Alex thought he probably had a whole closet full at home.

Mr. Hume taught what he called "practical arts," meaning he taught cooking and wood shop and arts and crafts and everything none of the other teachers wanted to teach. He had Alex's undying devotion because two years previously, he'd helped Alex get a model trebuchet to work, and, at least according to Alex, his knowledge of castles was unlimited. He once brought in a photo album of pictures of all the castles he'd visited—from Edinburgh Castle in Scotland ("too cold to go farther north") all the way to Windsor Castle in the south ("I couldn't afford train fair to go any further").

John had a brainwave at the end of lunch, just as they were lining up to go back to class.

"Let's ask Mr. Hume about the book." He whispered so none of the other students swirling around them could hear.

Since Mr. Hume was their last teacher of the day, they hung back until the other students left. Mr. Hume looked at them inquiringly, especially when they seemed hesitant about their errand.

"Uh, Mr. Hume," stammered John, who was always the one appointed to do difficult errands on behalf of the three. "Can you help us?"

"Of course! And what help could you need on your first day back at school?" Mr. Hume put down the art supplies he was picking up so he could give the boys his undivided attention. He sat on the edge of his desk to face them.

John told him about the book, at least everything except Marco, which John didn't think needed to be included. Alex provided more details about the trebuchet competition, but Conan shushed him. "And so, we need help opening the book."

"Didn't the fortuneteller give you the key?"

"No."

"Did you ask?"

"Well, Dad was sort of hurrying us along," admitted John, somewhat embarrassed by the question. After all, when handed a locked book, one should inquire about the key.

"And you say you've tried everything to cut the strap," repeated Mr. Hume, just to be sure.

"Everything. We were wondering if maybe you had an idea," asked Conan, speaking for the first time.

Mr. Hume rearranged his desk while thinking of a reply. He put the small tubes of paint back into a tub and dipped the brushes into a large jar of cloudy water.

"The only thing I can think of is the band saw."

"What's a band saw?" asked John and Conan at the same time.

Mr. Hume smiled. "I use it to cut shapes for tole painting. We'll be doing some in about a month."

"Where is it?" asked Alex, looking a little scared at the thought of a whole band of saws.

"It's in the basement in Old Hall," said Mr. Hume. "I'm afraid students aren't normally allowed in there. You probably won't see a band saw until your high school practical arts classes." He smiled conspiratorially. "It's a little dangerous. You have to use eye protection," he concluded, as though that proved the danger beyond doubt.

"Can you do it for us?" ventured John.

"Why don't you bring your book tomorrow and we'll try after school? I think there are enough eye protection goggles down there for all four of us."

"Wow!" exclaimed Alex. "So there really is a basement after all?"

"It's almost all taken up by the heating plant. But I've set up a little shop down there," said Mr. Hume. "I think it will be just right for a task as difficult as this." He winked at them conspiratorially.

Chapter 10

Alex was quite insistent. "It won't work!" he said as he and John watched Conan play a casual game of football after school. "The book is magic! We need a magic way to open it!"

"Right. Sure. But how?" John sat on the lowest seat of the bleachers and kicked at the grass.

Alex sat beside him. "I don't know yet. But I'll bet Mr. Hume knows magic, too! We can ask him tomorrow after school."

"He's never shown us any magic," countered John. "Whoa!" he exclaimed as the ball flew between his head and Alex's and bounced off the bleachers. Three players, a sixth year and two fifth years they didn't know, thundered past them to grab the ball.

"Are you sure we should be this close?" asked Alex. "We need some sort of magic phrase. Think back to what the old lady said."

"All I can remember is Marco yelling at us."

"She was muttering something when she looked into the crystal ball."

"I couldn't hear it," replied John as the players rushed past them, once again out of bounds. In a flash Conan picked up the ball and stepped on John's foot as he threw it back onto the pitch. He seemed completely oblivious to John's and Alex's earnest conversation.

"Can we please move higher? I'm going to get trampled," begged Alex.

Reluctantly, John stood and surveyed the bleachers. Alex bounded all the way to the top, about six rows up and sat down firmly, waiting for John to follow. John was on the second row when the ball came whizzing in their direction again. It bounced off row five and John caught it. He spun around and threw it back onto the pitch, where the whirling dervish snatched it up again. Conan could be identified only by his swirling ponytail.

"Maybe we could look up magic words on the Internet?" wondered John. "I don't know what it could be."

"Maybe Conan knows," mused Alex, looking down on the football game with distaste.

"Right now all Conan is thinking about is football," said John.

Chapter 11

John's schoolbag seemed particularly heavy all the next day, since stuffed at the bottom was the handwritten book. And the day dragged without end. Even lunch seemed to take a long time.

"Watch for Marco," said John to Conan while the latter was munching on his sandwich.

"Marco's not coming into the school grounds! Wouldn't be allowed," said Conan. "I want to play football after school again today. We've got some good players this year. Maybe we'll finally beat Alwoodley Primary. I'd like to do that before we go to high school."

"We're meeting Mr. Hume, remember?" said Alex. "Can I have your last carrot?"

Conan nudged the carrot in Alex's direction. "I hate carrots. Don't know why Mum gives them to me."

"Alex is right," said John. "You have to go with us." He shifted his schoolbag closer to his feet as a group of fourth-year girls came by, laughing at some private joke and pointing across the room. When some sixth year boys John never liked came by, he pulled his schoolbag up into his lap. The boys stood behind John to talk across the table to Conan about football, and that's where the conversation stayed for the rest of lunch while John and Alex finished their food in silence.

Even Mr. Hume's class seemed to go on forever. John kept his school bag near him, finally hooking one strap under his chair so no one could accidentally walk off with it. The class was about art collages, so everyone cut things out of magazines and pasted them onto an A2-sized piece of poster board. John tried hard to understand what Mr. Hume said about artistic composition, but nothing seemed to work out. Half sick with worry about the handwritten book, it was difficult to concentrate.

The bell rang at last. Half the class bolted for the door after putting away their supplies, but it seemed like the other half wanted the day to go on forever. It took 30 minutes before the classroom occupants were down to just John, Conan, Alex, and Mr. Hume.

"So where is this book?" asked Mr. Hume jovially.

John produced it from his school bag. Mr. Hume looked it over carefully, poking and prodding at the lock and bending the leather strap. "You're quite sure you want me to cut this strap?" he asked. Upon hearing a unanimous chorus from the boys, he rummaged deep into his desk drawer for a pair of scissors, but these were no match for the leather strap.

31

"It seems flexible enough. I'm sure the band saw will make short work of it!"

And with that, he handed the book back to John, who hastily stuffed it into his school bag. Mr. Hume led them out of the room, down the hall, out of New Hall, across the courtyard with its rosebushes, and into Old Hall. They paused outside the mysterious door marked 'Staff Only' while Mr. Hume rummaged in his pocket for a key. After a moment he pulled the door open.

"Students aren't normally allowed in here, so please be sure you don't touch anything. And step carefully." Mr. Hume snapped on a light, revealing a set of descending stairs.

The first thing that hit John's nose was the smell of coal dust mixed with sawdust. And it smelled of damp, too. John went first, followed by Conan and Alex, each descending into what looked like a dark cavern. Several passing students peered into the gloom. Mr. Hume pulled the door shut with a bang and followed the boys down the stairs. John stopped at the bottom of the stairs, staring into the darkness, not wanting to proceed until the main light was on.

Mr. Hume gently pushed past the boys and into the darkness, feeling along the wall. He found the switch and flipped it. The dimly-lit basement seemed to go on forever. In the very middle was a monstrous mechanical contraption. To the right was a large coal bin, full to the brim with small chunks of dusty coal. Some had spilled onto the floor. A chute went from the coal bin to the furnace. A giant screw down the middle pushed the coal into the furnace.

Along one wall were arrayed several large machines.

"This is a wood lathe—just got it last year," said Mr. Hume proudly. John thought it had too many handles. "And this is a table saw." This one seemed obvious to John—the saw blade was sticking up and it indeed looked like a table. "And the band saw is over here," he said, pointing to a funny-looking, rounded machine. "See, the blade is continuous. We just put your mysterious book on this little table here and turn it on. Won't take but a minute."

Mute, the boys stood around to watch. Mr. Hume confidently turned on the band saw, which whined at first and then hummed away. John fished in his school bag, pulled out the handwritten book, and handed it to Mr. Hume. "Here," said Mr. Hume. "Put on these goggles."

The boys adjusted the uncomfortable safety goggles. Once they were in place and Mr Hume checked them, they moved closer until Mr. Hume asked them to stand back a little bit. Mr. Hume put the book on the table and pressed it parallel to the saw blade. There was a rubbing sound as he pushed it against the blade.

"That's funny," he said, puzzled.

"What's funny?" asked Alex.

"It's not cutting," said Mr. Hume, pressing even harder.

"I told you," said Alex to John. "The book is magic!"

Mr. Hume pulled the book away, turned off the band saw and stepped on the brake to slow it down. He pushed his goggles onto his forehead, so all the boys, thinking this was the thing to do, did likewise. Mr. Hume ran his thumb over the edge of the strap.

"It didn't even leave a mark!"

He handed the book to John, who ran his thumb over the edge of the strap. John handed it to Conan, who also ran his thumb over the edge of the strap. And then Alex had his turn.

John broke the silence. "Can you use one of your other machines?"

Mr. Hume looked doubtful. "I suppose we can try the table saw. But stand back."

And so they stood back near the furnace. But it clicked mysteriously, so they moved to stand by the staircase. Mr. Hume started the table saw, which made a much bigger whine and seemed to hum with particular ferocity. He pulled his goggles down over his eyes and the boys did likewise without being told.

Mr. Hume tried it from every angle he could think of, pressing the book against the blade harder and harder. Occasionally he would rub his hand over the strap, and once he flexed it back and forth thoughtfully. And finally the saw blade caught the book in an odd way and ripped it out of Mr. Hume's hands and flung it across the basement floor, where it skidded to a halt just shy of the furnace. Mr. Hume jumped back in surprise and Alex shouted for no particular reason at all. John ran to the book and picked it up.

Once that happened, Mr. Hume turned off the table saw and waited for it to spin to a stop. "Sorry boys," he said. "It just won't cut."

"I told you," pronounced Alex. "The book is magic."

"Well, I don't know if it's magic," said Mr. Hume. "But it sure seems like it." He looked very puzzled.

Chapter 12

"Marco alert," whispered Conan as the three boys pushed open the door of Old Hall, leaving Mr. Hume in the shop down in the basement.

"Where?" exclaimed Alex, looking around wildly.

John clutched his school bag tighter. His stomach was suddenly in knots.

"He's behind the red car there, leaning up against the lamp post—see?" Conan pointed. "He has his back turned to us. But I saw his face for a second."

"Are you sure?" asked John, coming to a halt.

"Positive," affirmed Conan.

"We need a plan," said Alex. "He's standing by the only entrance to the school. Maybe we can get a disguise from Mr. Hume!"

So they went back inside Old Hall and banged on the locked door to the basement. They could hear the sound of the table saw, but no one answered their knocks. In fact, there was hardly anyone in the building. Conan's watch said 3:45 p.m.

"I have an idea," suggested Conan. "We can go down to the football pitch and wait for him to go away."

"You just want to play more casual football," said Alex.

"There's usually someone there until about five o'clock. We can wait him out."

No one had a better idea, so they left Old Hall and crossed the courtyard toward New Hall. Sure enough, Marco glanced across the street, then hastily averted his face, pretending to interest himself in someone's roses. John secretly hoped he would scratch his nose on the thorns.

The boys made their way through New Hall and came out the other end onto the athletic fields. They felt safe there, because the only way Marco could follow them there would be to enter the school grounds, and after much discussion all the way through New Hall, they had decided he would never dare do that.

And so John and Alex took up their positions atop the bleachers as Conan forgot all about the old book and thought of nothing but football. He was grabbed immediately by one of the groups out on the pitch, and soon all that could be seen of him in the sea of light blue shirts and navy trousers was his flying ponytail.

At 4:15, John sent Alex back through New Hall to peer into the courtyard to see if Marco was still there. Alex came back ten minutes later, huffing and puffing, to report that he was. The upsetting thing was that at first Alex didn't think he was there, so he went right up to the wrought iron fence that marked the boundary of the school property to peer through, and Marco walked up to him and said "I must talk to you!" And then Alex ran all the way back, which was considerable exertion for someone as small and bookish as Alex.

At 4:45, as the crowd of boys on the pitch was thinning, John took a gander himself, leaving his schoolbag with Alex. This time, he went into a first-year classroom that had windows that faced the front of the school and peered through the blinds. It took him five minutes to spot Marco, who was lounging outside the Clap Hammer Pub about a hundred yards down the High Street from the school.

By the time John returned to the bleachers, the boys had broken up their football game. Most needed to be out front at 5:00 p.m. so their parents could pick them up. Others, like John, Conan, and Alex, would be walking home.

"John!" called Conan. "Can you loan me 25 pence? I bet this guy I'd score before he did and he scored first. I don't have the money."

"You shouldn't bet! You always lose," said John, digging into his pocket and finding only 20p. Fortunately, Alex had a 5p. John paid the other boy, who was holding out his hand with a sneer and seemed bigger than Conan and Alex put together. Once paid, he turned and ran toward New Hall.

John and Alex told him Marco was still waiting outside.

"So do we run for it?" suggested Conan. "We could run to your house and get in before he could find us. I'll bet 25 pence he can't catch us!"

"You don't have any money left to bet," replied John. "And you owe me 20 pence. Is there a back way out of here?" He looked around, but nothing came to mind. The rugby pitch and the two football pitches were surrounded by a chain link fence which separated them from the flats on one side and some businesses at the other. At the far end of the rugby pitch, the fence disappeared behind several trees.

"Let's just walk along the boundary fence. Maybe there's a hole somewhere," suggested Alex. "It's like castles. They all had secret entrances."

"I don't think the school has a secret entrance," said John dryly. But after more discussion, they figured it was the only thing they could do. They decided if there was no other way out, they would ask one of the adults at the school to call the police, but that would mean telling them about the handwritten book.

So, they started walking down the fence in the direction of the rugby pitch. From the fence line, they could peer into the back gardens of the flats. Some were tidy, most were unkempt, and some were downright ragged. As they got to the end of the flats, they found something interesting. A gate had been put there, big enough to drive a truck through, probably to allow the gardener to get to the athletic fields. The gate was shut tight with a chain, but maybe....

Conan pushed gently. The gates swung open until the chain pulled tight. Whoever had put the chain back last time had not made sure it was tight.

"I think I can squeeze through. Here, push on the gates." It took him some strange contortions, but at last he had his head and torso through the gap. "Help me!" he said. "Push on the gate." And at last he was through, looking back through the gate at John and Alex.

"Well," said Conan. "I'm bigger than either of you. Push my school bag through."

They had to squash Conan's school bag flat to get it through the gate, but they succeeded. Then John squeezed through and pulled his precious school bag through. Alex slipped through easily, though his school bag took a little longer.

"Where are we?" asked Alex.

"I don't really know," said John. "This street comes out on the High Street where the school is."

"I don't like this place," said Conan.

The drive that led from the street to the gate was lined with several old, broken-down cars, one with a windshield that had been smashed to bits and two that each had four flat tires. Down at the end of the driveway, where it met the street, four teens smoked and laughed. One of them had a bottle he was sharing with the others.

"Maybe we should go back and take our chances with Marco," suggested Conan.

"No. We've got to go forward. Let's go down to the street," said John in the voice he used when he'd made up his mind. "But stick together."

And so they did. They tried not to look at the teens, even when one of them said something very rude indeed about primary school boys walking about unattended. John just stood a little taller and walked on, hoping the teens would leave them alone. After laughing and making some crude jokes at the boys' expense, including one about Conan's long hair, the teens' laughter receded behind them.

Rather than turn toward the High Street, John led Conan and Alex in the other direction. The street twisted away from the school and in the direction of central Manchester, whose skyscrapers they could see in the distance. The flats on either side of them, standing only three stories tall, seemed crowded. Unattended small children sometimes ran out to gawk at the three uniformed boys from Allerton Primary School, as though seeing someone in a school uniform this late in the day was unheard of.

37

And the sun was low on the horizon, compounding their problem. They could hear television sets blaring from the open windows on the warm evening. The smell of curry wafted across the street.

"Do you know where we are?" asked Alex anxiously as they passed another group of smoking teens. They endured another round of crude jokes, but this time the teens had things to talk about other than primary school children.

"I think that's the High Street up ahead," said John with a confidence he didn't feel.

They came out of the flats onto the High Street next to a loud pub called the Wheel's Hub. John glanced at his watch. It was 5:29 p.m.

"We could call Dad and have him come get us. But Mum and Dad don't get home until six o'clock," said John. "So we'll have to wait."

"My mum's still at work, and Dad…well…Dad is away," said Conan.

"We don't have a car," admitted Alex sheepishly.

They peeked inside the pub, but the Wheel's Hub seemed in need of oiling. It was already crowded and didn't look like the kind of place for boys whose combined age was less than that of most of the patrons. The bartender saw them peering in and came out to see what they were doing.

"What d'ya want?" he said threateningly. "You're underage, in case ya didn' notice."

"Please, sir," said John in his most polite voice. "Which way to Brixton Street from here?"

"You lost?"

"Not really," lied John. "We just ended up taking…you know…the long way around."

The bartender considered them for a minute, pausing to let in three more patrons. Behind him customers were yelling for another round of drinks.

"Ya a boy or girl?" he said, pointing at Conan.

"A boy," Conan replied fiercely, looking the publican straight in the eye.

"Hmph. Ya shouldn't be out at night, boys. Five blocks down there…"—he pointed—"…and turn left by the school." And with that, he turned and let the door clatter behind him.

"Girl!" muttered Conan. "What an idiot! Doesn't he ever watch Manchester United?"

"Come on. Let's go," said John.

They wended their way down the High Street in the gathering darkness. After crossing three streets, they recognized Allerton Primary School coming up on their right. They were back where they had started.

"I think we have the advantage," pointed out Alex. "He'll still be watching the gate. Maybe we can turn left one block early and come at your house from the other direction."

And so that is what they did. Conan, by now appointed the official Marco detector, kept swiveling his head. They walked the four-block length of Crewe Street four blocks, turned right onto Grantham Street, went one more block, and turned right again onto Brixton Street. Halfway down the block lay the Cunningham residence. It appeared empty except for two teens standing halfway down the block carrying on a loud conversation.

They started down the street, carrying their now-heavy school bags. They were fifty feet when Conan hissed "Marco alert!"

"Where?" hissed Alex.

"Down the street. A block away. Walking toward us."

They walked quickly and then ran the next few feet into the Cunningham driveway and onto the walk. The old Jaguar was in the driveway, but the lack of lights in the windows said no one was at home. John wondered where Katie was—probably at Susan's house. And Miriam would be across the street.

John pulled out his key and put it into the lock, but the door wouldn't budge.

"Hurry," hissed Alex.

John tried some more, wiggling the key back and forth.

"John, c'mon!" whispered Conan. "He's half a block away."

"I'm trying! Stupid door won't work!" whispered John in exasperation. He tried and tried and tried with increasing desperation.

"Hello boys," said Marco in an unctuous voice. "It's fortunate we meet again!"

John frantically kept trying the door key. He was beginning to sweat. Conan turned to face Marco while Alex tried to hide between Conan and John.

"What do you want?" challenged Conan. John kept working on the lock. It was close to getting well and truly dark, and the porch light was not on.

"I'm here to improve my offer to fifty pounds," said Marco, taking out his wallet. "I'm sure you would consider that very profitable."

"Why do you want the book?" said Conan while John jiggled the key again and again.

But Marco didn't answer directly. "Had you been able to open it, I'm sure you'd see that what it contains is far too advanced for you boys. I, on the other hand, would find it most useful. I'm afraid my wife never shared it with me. But," he said, suddenly threatening. "The book by rights belongs to me!" Less menacing, he continued. "Fifty pounds. I assure you, it's worth it." He moved closer. John was sweating so much his key ring was getting slippery in his trembling fingers, but still the door would not budge.

"Boys! Why aren't you in the house? You should've been home ages ago! And who's this with y…oh my!"

John breathed a great sigh and ceased struggling with the door. The voice belonged to Dad! He turned around to see his father and mother standing behind Marco.

Marco spoke first. "I'm simply here to improve my offer for the book."

Dad spoke second. "How did you learn where we live! I'll call the police! You're stalking us!"

Mum spoke third. "Wait! Mr. Marco, if that is indeed your name, if the boys change their minds, how do we contact you?"

"Mum! What? We're not selling!—At any price!" exclaimed John.

"The book is magic!" exclaimed Alex.

Marco seemed thunderstruck. "How did you know?" he stammered.

"You are stalking these boys!" said Dad. "You will leave at once and never return!"

"Have you opened it?" asked Marco, who seemed thoroughly amazed.

"Yes!" shouted Alex. "And it's full of magic! We're never selling it! Go away!"

"Oh no! Please, please! Give me the book!" Marco looked as though he was begging.

"Wait!" commanded Mum. "Mr. Marco—if the boys change their minds, how do we contact you?"

But Marco seemed disoriented.

"How do we contact you," insisted Mum, taking a note pad out of her bag.

"Just leave a message for me at the Clap Hammer Pub," Marco finally stammered.

"Now be gone!" commanded Dad. "If we see you around here again, we'll call the police. Leave these boys alone! Do not contact them in any way!"

Muttering distractedly under his breath, Marco wandered aimlessly down the walk. He stopped at the street and looked at the boys. "I'll have that book!" he said, and then walked briskly down the street in the direction from which he'd come.

"Boys, get inside," said Dad. "I want to hear what happened."

"Dad, the lock won't work."

"Let me try," said Dad. He took out his key and tried it in the lock. The door opened effortlessly.

Chapter 13

Well, Dad was pretty grumpy when he heard the whole story. He decided to call the police anyway. They promised to check out Marco, but thought the hopes were slim if the only clue was that he could be found via the Clap Hammer.

Mum defended her question by saying it was the only way to find out anything about him, though of course he hadn't told him much. Mum was unnerved by his parting comment.

John decided after it was all over and they'd eaten dinner that perhaps he shouldn't go wandering into other neighborhoods after school.

41

Conan was something of the hero for having spotted Marco so early, but was still confused as to how Marco knew which street to walk up to meet them.

And Alex was in trouble for lying to Marco. He positively bristled at Dad's suggestion that honesty is always the best policy. "But now we know the book is magic!" he exclaimed. "And we *will* get it open! We just need to think of the right words!"

Dad looked at the handwritten book and marveled that a band saw and a table saw made no impression on the leather. "It seems flexible enough," he said. "I don't know why we can't cut it."

"Because it's magic!" insisted Alex.

Chapter 14

Over the next several weeks the boys gathered often in John's bedroom after school and on weekends. Alex tried all the magic words he could think of.

"Abracadabra!"

"Alakazam!"

"Jiggery-pokery!"

"Presto!"

But nothing happened.

He tried holding it over his head, behind his back, under his feet, and between his knees.

Nothing.

John and Conan were losing interest, but humored Alex as the days wore on. The autumn weather pattern was moving into the Manchester area, so there were days when they ran to school because Alex said they'd get less wet that way. And the winds were chilly, too. One day the wind tore the big umbrella right out of John's hand and they had to chase it across the street.

The book, meanwhile, was hidden under John's mattress. At first he put it right under the middle, but that only lasted about fifteen minutes after John went to bed, since it made a great big lump in the middle of the bed. So he moved it so it was under the mattress right next to where the bed was pushed against the wall. He thought this was still very secure, because if anyone sneaked into the room, they'd have to lean over John to get to it, which would alert him so he could defend the book. A couple nights he had dreams in which people did exactly that, but he'd always wake up to find no one in the room. He didn't need a night light to tell, because the street lamp made his room very bright anyway.

Chapter 15

The weather on Halloween was particularly nasty. The boys hid themselves in their warmest jackets and sweaters to make their way to school. Allerton Primary School did essentially nothing to celebrate Halloween because a big committee of parents had objected the previous year, but this did not keep Alex from being excited.

"Halloween is for magic! Today's the day! I just know it!"

"And how do you know it?" asked Conan as they crossed the High Street to go into the school, passing through the wrought-iron gate.

"I just know it."

And that's all they could get out of him all day.

At John's suggestion, both Conan and Alex would be at the Cunninghams for dinner that evening. The thought of this simply made Alex more excited, because he planned to spend the evening working on the handwritten book rather than dressing in costume, though John and Conan worked hard all day to dissuade him.

"We've tried everything!" said Conan.

"It'll never open. There are no such things as flying broomsticks," said John.

Although Mum and Dad had been invited to a fancy dress party at Dad's work, they had opted to stay home so that Mum could deal with children coming to the door and Dad could accompany the three boys on their rounds in costume. But Mum insisted first they would have tea, and so the three excited boys sat at the big round table in the kitchen along with Mum and Dad and Katie and Miriam. Although the lasagna came from a frozen box, Mum had made corn muffins following a recipe her cousin in America had e-mailed to her.

"Pass the muffins," said John to Katie.

Katie didn't budge. She said she was too old for Halloween nonsense and seemed in a particularly bad mood.

John rose to the bait, just as any little brother would. "Katie! Pass the muffins!"

Mum sensed an argument in the making and moved to intervene. "Katie, dear..." she began.

"He didn't say the magic word, mum! He's always bossing me around. Tell him to stop!"

"And what's the magic word?" asked Alex eagerly. He put down his fork and picking up a muffin before the tray was passed out of his reach.

"It's 'please,' dummy," responded Katie sullenly.

"What!" expostulated Alex. "That's a magic word?"

"Don't you ever say 'please' at home?" Katie responded, giving him a withering look.

"Of course I...wait a minute!...I'll be right back!" He pushed back his chair, threw his napkin to the floor, and rushed to John's room. John could hear his door being opened with such force it bounced off the wall, something Mum was always telling him not to do. Alex's head shot into the hallway. "Where's the book?"

John reluctantly got to his feet, careful to put his napkin on his chair rather than let it fall to the floor. "Don't tear the room apart. I'll get it." He made his way quickly down the hall before Alex could cause irreparable harm. He groped for the light switch in the hallway, tripped over the throw rug, and threw himself into his room. Alex was groping through John's bed, so John turned on the light.

"Hold on!" commanded John. "Just a minute! You're tearing the bed apart!"

Pushing a feverish Alex back, John pulled back the mattress and retrieved the handwritten book, snug in its hiding place. He started to dust lint off, but Alex grabbed it and ran back into the kitchen. John followed him, but walked instead of ran.

"Conan!" shouted Alex. "Stand here with us!"

"Don't shout, Alex!" shouted Conan, but nevertheless he pushed back from the table and joined John and Alex in standing in a little circle around the book.

44

"This will work! I know it will! Okay, each of you put your hands under the book, just like mine. Hold onto it with your thumbs on top."

"Why?" asked John and Conan at the same time.

"Just do it. I saw a picture of this in an old book in the school library. Thumb on top, Conan!"

"Okay," said Conan. "Now what?"

"I think we all need to close our eyes. Ready? Here goes. Please open!"

Nothing seemed to happen—they didn't hear anything magic or see flashes of light. Disappointed, they all opened their eyes.

"Are you sure that would work?" asked John.

"Try the latch," said Alex simply.

By this time Mum and Dad joined them. Dad looked curious, but Mum was suspicious. Dad put his forefinger out and tugged at the latch.

It fell away with a little click.

Chapter 16

"Yoohoo!" shouted Alex! "I knew it!" And he proceeded to do a war dance around the room, pumping his tiny fist in the air. "'Please' was the magic word!"

"Open it!" shouted Conan.

"Don't shout," muttered Miriam. "What's the big deal?"

"Yes, open it," said Dad in a much more reasonable tone. "Let's see what all this fuss has been about."

So John sat at the table and pushed his half-eaten and now forgotten plate back to make room and heaved the book up where he could open it. Alex and Conan crowded behind him. Dad stood behind them.

John opened the cover. The first page was handwritten to look like a title page.

All the Magic I've Ever Learned

By Miriam Stoney

And that was all that was on the first page.

"So this is a really old book!" said Conan, reaching out to touch the book and urge John to turn the page. "Miriam must be that old lady's name!"

"I don't like her having the same name as me!" exclaimed Miriam. She shivered a little.

"Oh, I don't think fifty years is all that old," said Mum. "Your aunt is much older than that!"

"Are you going to turn the page?" asked Conan, prodding the book.

So John turned the page. The next page looked like a list of subjects that the old woman thought might be important. Each of the subjects had a page number. At the bottom were several subjects that had no page numbers, so perhaps she had never written them.

Fortune Telling (Crystal Balls) 3

Arithmancy 18

Cartomancy 29

Flying Broomsticks 41

Disappearing and Invisibility 65

Healing salves 83

Magic Wands 125

Immunity to curses

Simple tricks to impress

And the list went on for several other subjects that had no page numbers. John flipped through the book and saw cramped handwriting and meticulous drawings in many different colors of ink, some faded with age. Here and there were stains on the paper, as though the old lady had dropped something on them. Once in a while, pages were stuck together.

"Turn to the section on broomsticks," squealed Alex. "That's what she wanted us to build. She said she saw us flying a broomstick."

"I don't like her using my name," repeated Miriam.

"Now, now, dear," said Mum. "Miriam is a very pretty name."

"I bet she was ugly," complained Miriam.

"She was, kind of," confirmed Conan, which made Miriam wilt in her seat.

"I don't want to be ugly when I grow up!" she wailed.

"I didn't mean you're ugly!" said Conan. "I just said the old lady was ugly."

"Boys, Miriam, enough!" said Dad.

John turned to Page 41, marked in old-fashioned, greenish printed numbers in the corner of the page. Conan and Alex were pressing on his back so hard they were pushing his face down onto the book.

"Careful!" he muttered.

The instructions looked seriously complicated. Page 41 was devoted to an illustration of an old witch in a flowing black cape and a pointed, broad-brimmed hat standing next to a broomstick which presumably flew. The illustration had lots of arrows and explanations, all in tiny handwriting. As John flipped through the next several pages, it became even more complicated. Two pages were devoted to finding just the right broom handle, which had to be made of ash. Then the twigs had to be gathered, and these could be both birch and willow. In a pinch, broom straw would do, but was said to make an inferior broom. And the twigs had to be fastened to the broom handle just so. Page 48 was devoted to dire warnings about what happened if the broom were not made properly, and listed the deaths of Mary Banks of Kent, Phyllis Carmody of Sussex, and Walter Smithson of Glasgow, all attributed to not paying attention to detail while making their broom.

Finally John looked up at his father. "I can't read half the handwriting and this looks really complicated."

Dad moved over for a closer look, finally picking the book up from the table to flip through its pages.

"Don't put the latch back in!" shouted Alex.

"Alex, you shout too much," complained Miriam. "How come I don't get to see?"

But Dad ignored them both and flipped through the pages, scanning the illustrations.

"It looks pretty complicated, boys," he said. "Are you sure you want to try this? It'll take hours and hours."

"For sure!" squeaked Alex.

"I suppose," said Conan.

"Can I see, Dad?" asked John.

Dessert forgotten, John started thumbing through the section on flying broomsticks. It was divided into four sections. One detailed broomstick history, starting in the Middle Ages in 1202 when a magician by the name of Olgen found he could make objects levitate. This he passed on to his student Milven, who figured out how to make a broomstick fly. There was lots more history, but John skimmed through this. Next was a section on the theory of broomstick flight, which made reference to levitation, the fundamental elements of earth, air, fire, and water, and dire warnings to do things in the right order else the results would be unpredictable. The third section, comprising some fifteen pages of diagrams and more cramped handwriting, described how to build a broomstick. It looked exceptionally complicated. And the fourth and final section described how to fly a broomstick, with one final short paragraph at the end about more than one person flying the same broomstick at once, what it called "tandem flying."

"So what do we have to do first?" asked Alex, munching on his dessert of apple crumb cake and grabbing the book.

John held tight. "Blimey! It's seriously complicated! It's not like just making any old broomstick fly. It has to be made perfectly. Looks weird."

Dad took the book back and flipped through the section. "It's full of warnings," he said. "I think you'd best be careful. Get Mr. Hume to help you." Dad knew that Mr. Hume was their favorite teacher. "Doesn't Mr. Hume have a wood shop at Allerton?"

"We went down there," said Conan proudly. "Normally students aren't allowed!"

"Yeah," replied Alex. "Kind of spooky in the basement. The lights aren't very good."

Dad was still flipping pages. "There's something in here about needing to take it to a specific castle in order to make it work. But I've never heard of Castle Alox. Very strange name. I think I would remember it, but I don't know of a castle by that name."

"Mr. Hume will know where it is!" said Alex with great assurance. "He knows every castle in the world!"

"In England, you mean," said Conan, helping himself to more apple crumb cake.

"Same thing," muttered Alex.

"Don't let the Germans and French hear you say that," said Mum. "John, dear, are you going to have any dessert?"

"Yes," said John, startled back into reality. "Hey, Conan! That's my dessert you're taking!"

Chapter 17

Finally Mum told them that if they were going to go from house to house for trick or treat, they'd better get going. Alex wanted to stay to look at the book, but John put his foot down and reminded him the book would be there when they got back. But even John wouldn't leave until Dad had wrapped some cloth tape around the end of the clasp so it couldn't accidentally hook back into the latch, leaving them with a closed book. John wasn't sure how many times simply saying "please" would work.

Alex was dressed as a skeleton, which made him look even smaller than he was. Conan dressed in a Manchester United jersey with the name and number of his favorite player emblazoned on the front and back and asked Mum to make sure his ponytail looked exactly like his hero's. John was dressed in a long black cape and a pointed, broad-brimmed hat, which he told people was like a male witch, although he preferred the term 'wizard.' Porch lights were on at about a third of the houses, and they collected candy for about an hour before their curiosity about the handwritten book forced them back home.

Alex poured his candy out on the big round table in the kitchen to take inventory. "So do you think there's real magic?" he asked.

"No!" said Conan. "It's only in the movies and old fairy tales."

John spoke up. "So you think making a flying broomstick will be impossible, then…."

"I didn't say that," replied Conan. "It's interesting, though. Why couldn't we cut through the latch, but just saying 'please' made the book open?"

"It's magic!" said Alex. "I only got two Mars bars. Some of this isn't even candy! Look—someone gave me a toothbrush!"

"I got one of those, too," said Conan. "Someone's idea of a bad joke, I suppose. We should go back there with eggs."

"I don't remember which house it was."

"Boys, you can skip the eggs," chided Mum. "How was the haul this year?"

"Sorry, Mrs. Cunningham. Just joking!" said Conan hastily.

"Can we look at the book again before we have to leave?" begged Alex.

So John carefully returned all his candy to his bag and trod the familiar path down the hallway and past the family pictures to his room. He stashed the candy in his dresser, changed his mind, opened the drawer and removed a chocolate bar and then closed the drawer again. He crawled onto his bed and pulled the handwritten book out from under the mattress.

John was not the only one enjoying the feast. Conan was working on a small bag of toasted almonds and Alex had opted for the same kind of chocolate bar as had John. John plopped the book on the big round table in the kitchen. Katie was doing her homework on one side of the big round table and wasn't pleased with the interruption. Miriam was in the sitting room watching television, so that left a little more space.

"Can't you guys find anywhere else to look at that stupid book?" asked Katie, annoyed. "There's no such thing as magic! It'll be a waste of time."

"Go back to your homework," said John.

"What about *your* homework?" interrupted Katie.

"I'll do it after Conan and Alex leave."

"Children," warned Mum, who was busy at the sink. "There's room for everybody."

Katie stuck out her tongue when Mum wasn't looking. John, Conan and Alex ignored her and crowded around the book.

They studied the book, with John pointing out the sections he'd seen previously on history, theory, construction, and flying. Conan wasn't interested in history or theory, but wanted to go straight to construction. Over Alex's objections, they did.

"I don't think we can do this ourselves," said Conan after they'd all read over each other's shoulder. Katie glared at them whenever they spoke aloud, and she was glaring at them now.

"You're knocking the table about," she said irritably. "It's making my handwriting sloppy."

"That's nothing new. Probably an improvement," said John. "I think..." but Mum cast them a quelling glance.

"Anyway, what I'm saying is we're going to have to show this to Mr. Hume tomorrow. We need his help!"

"I'll bet," said Katie nastily, "that you build this thing and it'll never work. And then I'll say I told you so!"

"Shut up, Katie!" exclaimed Alex, with a vehemence that startled even John.

Chapter 18

When John bid adieu to his friends and closed the door, he was torn. Katie could be right, after all. What if they followed the complicated instructions and nothing happened? But it just couldn't be! After all, it had taken a magic word, even if it was something so simple as 'please,' to open the book where a band saw and a table saw had failed. And, after all, Marco wanted the book so badly that he came all the way to Manchester in his bid to take it away from them, even offering them £50, which looked to be his life's savings. What was going on?

51

Reluctantly, he put the book back in its hiding place under the mattress. He couldn't help thinking it wasn't a truly secure place —after all, the house was vacant during the day while Mum and Dad were at work and the children were at school. Maybe they should get a safe? Maybe the book should be kept down at the bank, where they had an imposing, gleaming vault that bristled with security, not to mention armed guards.

And though John sat at the big round table in the kitchen with his own homework, he couldn't concentrate. Even his math homework, which was normally fairly easy, seemed insurmountable. He had to ask Dad for help. And for his science class, he answered the questions but put off the essay until the next day, finally giving up on homework as a bad job.

"Now, dear," said Mum to John as she clanked some dishes on the sink. "Just because you've opened that handwritten book, you must remember you have your schoolwork to do. Schoolwork comes first!"

"Yes, Mum."

"No, John. Really. You can talk with Mr. Hume about the book tomorrow. In the meantime, just put it out of your mind." She went back to drying a pot with a white dish towel.

"It's not that easy," said John. "Mum, do you think there is really any magic?"

She put down her towel and sat beside John, looking him in the eye.

"I don't know. I rather think not, to tell you the truth. If there were really magic, why don't we see more of it?"

"I remember once you told me electricity was like magic," insisted John.

She took hold of his hand, laying it on the table. "Yes, that was a long time ago, when you could barely read. But scientists understand lots of things about electricity. We use electricity for everything! But we don't need magic words. We just flip on the light and pay our bill every month." She was speaking in her gentle voice, the one she used when she didn't want John to be upset.

"But how come we were finally able to open the book with a simple word?" asked John, feeling rather like the time years ago when his father took his teddy bear away from him and set it on the high dresser, telling him he was too old to be carrying it about anymore.

"I don't know. Maybe it's magic," said Mum, biting her lip and caressing John's hand. "Or maybe after all the work you boys did, it finally jarred loose."

"But the old lady—Miriam—worked so hard to write everything down. Why would she work so hard if it was all made up?"

"John," she said, rather relishing his name. "She's a fortune-teller. Maybe she really believed it. From what you said she's really good at what she does. But maybe most of it is just stuff that was handed down. Like legend."

"Legend," repeated John. "You mean like King Arthur?"

"Yes, things like that. We all want to believe in fairy tale worlds, but it's just that they're such good stories they get passed down through the generations."

"But I thought there really was a King Arthur," objected John, looking at his mum carefully, for she seemed to be in a very unusual mood.

"Some people think so, and some people don't. There's no proof either way," she said with a faraway look. "I loved stories of King Arthur when I was a girl. Maybe that's why I like Alex so much. When I was ten I knew all about castles and knights and princes and princesses and could spout the Arthurian Legend from memory." She took her hand off John's and ran it through her hair. "I used to imagine myself as Guinevere."

"Who's that?" asked John.

She just smiled. "Ask Alex," she said. "Look, John. I know this handwritten book seems very exciting. But your schoolwork comes first. Maybe learning what this old woman wants you to know about magic can be your hobby for a while, but your schoolwork will determine your future." She had a note of finality in her voice. "Have you finished your homework?"

"Yes, Mum," muttered John, knowing it was pointless to say any more.

"I love you, John," she said.

Startled, John looked at her. He always knew Mum loved him, but she was not the type to say it very often, usually on his birthday and at Christmas or at other special times.

"I love you too, Mum," he stammered. He picked up his homework off the big round table and put it into his school bag and stood to leave the kitchen, but before he could gain the door, she swept him into a hug.

This seemed most unlike Mum.

Chapter 19

John put his schoolbag on the floor next to his dresser. He donned his pajamas and put his dirty clothes in the hamper in the hallway, turned on his bedside lamp and turned off the overhead lamp. The hardwood floor felt cold on his feet, but his Mum wouldn't let him sleep with socks, saying his feet needed a chance to "breathe during the night." Right now it felt like the phrase was "freeze during the night," because even with the central heating which had been installed before they bought the house, John's room always seemed chilly.

He crawled under the covers, shivering and waiting for his body heat to warm the cold bedclothes. This was why he hated going to bed. Of course, the bedclothes were snuggly and warm in the morning, which is why he hated getting out of bed, too. But that wouldn't happen until his rusty alarm clock told him it was time, and that seemed a long ways away at the moment. He reached for the bedside lamp to turn it off, but on an impulse left it on. He dug under the mattress for the handwritten book and pulled it out. Propping up his pillows, he set out to discover more about Miriam Stoney, who had started work on this diary more than 50 years before.

The old woman, it turned out, must not have been that old when she started the book, figured John. She certainly had looked to be at least a hundred in that tent, but on reflection, Aunt Emma was in her 80s and probably about the same age. Miriam Stoney wrote very little about herself, just a few words here and there, since it was clear this was intended to be a textbook on magic. But, by flipping through the first section on fortune telling, it appeared Ms. Stoney was 18 years old when she and her 16-year-old brother Marco had run off with the circus in Nottingham to escape her "dreadful parents" whom, according to the handwritten book, had beaten the two of them regularly. John thought this was interesting. Clearly Marco had lied when he said the old woman was his wife. No wonder she thought she could give it to whom she pleased.

Marco Stoney worked with the animals in the circus, seeming to have a particular talent with the lions and tigers. Miriam Stoney, on the other hand, found an old fortune teller who was happy to have a beautiful young assistant to draw in the crowd. At first, wrote Ms. Stoney, the instructions were simple—observe something about the customer and make up a very general fortune after appearing to peer into the crystal ball.

But as she gained more experience and the circus moved from place to place, she thought she could see real things in the crystal ball. The old fortune teller encouraged her in this, giving her instructions about letting her mind go and how to hold the crystal ball to make the images more clear. With several years of practice, she was giving very specific fortunes and started attracting the attention of people who'd line up to get their fortunes told. Once in a while she made mistakes, including one where she'd told a young man to invest in a particular stock. The investment proved disastrous, and the young man was most unhappy. This gave her some trouble with the police, so after that she refused to give prognostications about anything having to do with money, though once in a while she made an exception when the crystal ball seemed particularly clear.

After that, the old fortune teller introduced Miriam Stoney to some old people indeed who taught her more magic.

True magic seems so rare and yet so delightful. I simply do not understand why more people don't pay attention. They are either afraid of it and demonize it, or else they embrace the concept, trying to make a religion of it, without ever learning the old magic that actually works. I fear true magic will die of neglect, and so I am undertaking this great project to write down everything I know or can find out in the hope it will be passed along to someone willing enough to believe it and try it. A person is not born with magic. Rather, it is a skill, acquired with great patience at the feet of those who have learned it well. There are those who don't want me to pass it on. I'm rather afraid my brother is in that latter category, thinking magic is to be somehow protected. But if no one learns magic, there is nothing to protect it from!

John turned the page, determined now to read the history of flying broomsticks, when his mother came into the room.

"I saw your light on when I got up for a glass of water," she said gently. "It's nearly two o'clock in the morning! There will be another night! Let me turn off your light for you, dear."

And with no light, he couldn't read any more.

Chapter 20

School seemed to drag the next day, for several reasons. First, John was tired—extremely so. Second, they had to wait all day before they could see Jack Hume. And third, John once again had the handwritten book with him, which was heavy, plus now that it was open and they knew what was inside of it, John, Conan and Alex were all jumpy that someone might make a grab for it.

"Why'd you stay up so late reading it?" asked Conan as they were walking past the second year art classroom.

"Why didn't you stuff a towel at the bottom of your door so your mum couldn't see and then read some more?" asked Alex as they came upon some third years lining up for class.

"Don't give me such a hard time. I'm sleepy," replied John as they neared the cafeteria.

But Alex wouldn't give up. "If you're not going to read it, can I?" he chimed in as they walked inside the cafeteria. Conan, again with a sack lunch, went to stake a claim for table space while John and Alex continued the conversation.

"Why don't you come over to our house in the evening and read it?" asked John while they jostled in the noisy line and drew green trays from the holder. "You can read it while I do my homework."

"I've got homework too," said Alex. "Why do we do everything at your house, anyway?"

"I don't like the look of the sandwiches today. I want something warm. I've been cold all day," complained John.

"So why do we do everything at your house?" repeated Alex, determined to get an answer.

"I don't know," replied John. "We always have. Forever. Maybe it's because Mum always has food around."

Alex was silent and seemed moody for a moment, at least that's the way he seemed to John, so much so that John turned to stare at him.

Alex was shaken out of his reverie when a fifth-year girl asked him if he was ever going to get some food. Alex ordered the shepherd's pie and turned to John and said in a low voice so no one else could hear.

"I wish I had a father."

John didn't know what to say. Alex had never complained to him before about family matters. John had always taken it for granted that he had a mother and a father. And sisters, though he wasn't always certain he was glad he had those. Now that he thought about it, Alex and Conan both spent enormous amounts of time at his house—nearly every day, in fact. Sometimes they stopped by after school just to hang around. It seemed like Mum invited them to stay for dinner at least once a week, sometimes more. Mum seemed to pay particular attention to Alex. John suspected she talked with Conan's and Alex's mums, but never said anything about this to him.

John said nothing. He paid for his lunch and waited for Alex to pay for his, then the two of them made their way through the noisy crowd to where Conan was sitting.

Chapter 21

"This looks seriously complicated," said Mr. Hume, looking through the handwritten book while seated at the desk in the arts and crafts classroom. The boys had gathered around behind him to peer over his shoulder.

"Dad said that too. What's so complicated?" asked John.

Mr. Hume took his time answering. He turned the pages in the 'how to build it' section on broomsticks back and forth, occasionally turning the book sideways to read one of the figures.

"I thought it would simply be a case of attaching some broom straw to a stick and then you would have something you could call a flying broomstick. But this requires a particular type of wood—ash—that's not the easiest to get. In fact, I don't think I've ever seen it as a round pole—always flat boards. It's definitely a hardwood. It says here it's best if it's carved directly from a branch. I don't know how we're going to do that. I get most of my wood from a dealer in Stockport who has a pretty wide selection, but I've never seen ash as a pole."

John's heart started to sink. "Does it say we can do it any other way? Maybe we can use a fence post or something."

Mr. Hume smiled. "You have two choices. You can follow these instructions exactly, which will be hard, or else you can make something that looks just like it, using much less expensive materials."

"But then will it fly?" asked Alex, wary.

"Boys," said Mr Hume, settling back in his chair. "I've seen lots of things in my life. When I was in the Army I went all over the world. But—and I'm being very honest here—I've never seen any real magic."

"But what about when you couldn't open the book?" chimed in Conan, speaking for the first time since class had ended.

Mr. Hume was thoughtful. He looked at the leather strap. "How did you boys get the book open, anyway?"

"By saying the magic word," piped Alex. "It was simple! We just said 'please.'"

Mr. Hume smiled accommodatingly, clearly trying not to stamp on Alex's enthusiasm. "But are you sure saying 'please' just didn't happen to coincide with jarring the mechanism in just the right way?"

"I'm positive!" stated Alex.

"I think he may be right," said John. "In any event, we want to build the broomstick the way it says in the book."

"So where do we find an ash pole?" asked Conan.

"How big does it have to be?" asked John at the same time.

Mr. Hume looked at the book again and answered John's question first. "The pole needs to be seven feet long for multiple riders, if I read this correctly." He turned the book sideways again. "As for ash poles, I suppose you need to contact a lumber dealer. I can give you the phone number of my favorite place in Stockport. It looks..."—he referred to the diagram again—"...as though the pole can be bent slightly, but it recommends that it be as straight as possible. And it says absolutely no bark can remain on the pole."

"Can't we just get a dead limb from an ash tree or something?" asked Conan, peering over Mr. Hume's shoulder at the book.

"Well, I suppose that would be a last resort. It says 'seasoned ash,' meaning wood that's thoroughly dried out. Plus, ash is a hardwood, so it's not just a matter of cutting it up. You need a sawmill to do it. And a proper lathe to make the pole. Seven feet means a bigger lathe than I have—mine will only do four feet—I use it to make table legs, which don't have to be all that long."

"What else do we need?" asked John.

"For the broom end you need twigs from either birch or willow," said Mr. Hume. "If you want, I know a good place to get broom straw. I'm going to use some in a fourth-year class project in a couple months, so I could just get some more for you."

"Does the book allow broom straw?" asked Alex suspiciously.

"It discourages it, but if you're just trying to make a look-alike broom..."

"No!" exploded Alex. "We've got to do it just right, or it won't work!"

Mr. Hume smiled. "Well, then, you should be able to gather the twigs you need. The book suggests a ratio of 40 birch twigs to every 55 willow twigs. Oh, and there's more. The twigs are bound to the broom by linen yarn—maybe your mum can come up with that. And, get this. The yarn has to be wound onto the broom along with the twigs in a very specific way."

"So? Then that's what we'll do!" said Alex emphatically.

Even John had to smile at Alex's enthusiasm. He had the distinct impression that Mr. Hume was just humoring them—that he didn't think they'd carry through with the project.

"Mr. Hume," said John. "Once we've built this broom, how do we make it fly? According to the book, that is. I couldn't quite figure that part out."

Mr. Hume looked at it some more. He couldn't help but grin. "You have to wrap a freshly-killed garden snake around the broomstick and place the broom at the top of the North Tower at Castle Alox within three hours of midnight, within three days of the full moon. And you need to cover it with the entrails of a freshly-killed goat. You'll know if it'll fly if there is a bolt of lightning during that time period."

"So where's Castle Alox?" asked Alex.

"No idea," said Mr. Hume. John thought Mr. Hume was trying to find a nice way of discouraging them from the entire project. "I've never heard of the place. It gives a drawing of the castle, though. Perhaps Alox is just a code name or something. See the picture?"

The boys crowded around the desk so they could get a look. The drawing showed a crenelated castle tower several stories tall on the corner of a large, square building. The drawing showed a portion of the moat and the castle drawbridge.

"So if this is the north tower, this must be the west wall, right?" ventured Conan.

"Exactly," responded Mr. Hume. "It doesn't appear to be all that big, perhaps three stories tall. I don't know any castles that look like it, but there are so many castles in Britain I could easily have missed one. Unless…."

"Yes!" said Alex eagerly.

"We don't know how long this information has been handed down. The diary itself is fifty years old. What if the old castle has been torn down?"

"But we've got to have at least the North Tower!" objected Alex. "Otherwise this won't work!"

Mr. Hume sighed. "Sorry to be disappointing, Alex, but we don't even know if this Castle Alox is in England. The construction in the picture certainly looks like that of English castles—perhaps Welsh or southern Scotland, but it could also be Ireland. I'm afraid your Miriam Stoney isn't that detailed as an artist. See the perspective here?" He traced a line with his finger. "That's the way they drew in the Middle Ages. I suspect this has been copied from an old manuscript."

"So," said Conan. "Let's assume at least the North Tower is still standing. We just have to look at pictures of old castles on the web until we find it." He looked dubious. "Right?" he asked.

"Not every castle has a website," replied Mr. Hume. "Some are protected by the National Trust. Others are in private hands and are off-limits to explorers. And others are so ruined you can just barely make out the foundation walls. I'd say you have quite a search on your hands."

"I guess the question we really want to ask is whether you'll help us build a broomstick," asked John. "One that follows these instructions."

Mr. Hume smiled while he surveyed them. John felt as though he was being sized up. Mr. Hume looked particularly hard at Alex as though seeing right through him. Alex stared back. Conan looked quietly confident, as though dealing with goat entrails was something he did every day.

"Okay, boys. You're on."

Chapter 22

John, Conan and Alex figured it would be easy to find a piece of ash. That evening they met in the Cunningham kitchen around the big round table after Conan and Alex had been invited to stay for dinner. Dad seemed surprised that Mr. Hume volunteered to help them.

"You're sure you want to do this?" he asked.

"Positively!" beamed Alex, who was holding the handwritten book.

"Your schoolwork comes first," repeated Dad, for about the fifth time during the conversation.

"We just need to find the supplies. Mr. Hume will help us put them together."

Dad hauled the telephone book down from the top of the refrigerator. The Manchester telephone book is thick because the Manchester Metroplex is big. Conan grabbed the book. Dad directed him to look up lumber yards and specialty wood dealers, because finding a two-inch thick, seven-foot long ash pole was going to be difficult, he said.

It was too late to call dealers that late at night, so the next day after school the boys ran home. Well, Conan ran. John held back a bit because of Alex. And Alex took up the rear, exhausted from so much physical activity and unable to keep up.

So they started calling all the lumberyards and specialty wood dealers. For call after call, they found the same answer: ash comes in one-inch thick boards and was very expensive, since it's used to make fine furniture. No one seemed to have ash poles, especially one that was two inches in diameter and seven feet long.

They sighed when they looked at the list. They hadn't even finished going through the A's when it was time for tea, and there was no point in calling after tea, because by then the shops were closed. They found that lumberyards were not generally open in the evening.

One store offered oak, but only as shovel handles. Another store tried to get them to buy pine. Still another suggested gluing pieces of ash together and putting them in a lathe, which they volunteered to do for a hundred pounds.

And Dad was as good as his word, insisting their schoolwork come first, and seemed particularly grumpy when John brought home a note from a teacher that said he didn't always seem to be paying attention. And football had started at school, which meant that Conan was often required to stay after for practice.

By mid November, they were only into the F's. And they were getting discouraged.

"I don't think you'll find an ash pole in a regular lumber yard," said Mr. Hume. "Have you tried the specialty woods store in Stockport I told you about?"

"Uh..." said Alex.

"Uh..." stammered Conan.

"No," finished John.

"We forgot," mumbled Alex. He stared down at Mr. Hume's desk. They'd now lost four weeks and had made no progress. "Could we have the number again? I don't think it's in the Manchester phone book."

Mr. Hume smiled. He pulled the top right hand drawer opened and started rummaging around, fishing through spare art brushes, pots of paint, newspaper clippings, student handouts, and glue bottles. "Here it is," he said at last, fishing out a business card. "I thought I had their card here." He handed it to Alex, who promptly handed it to John.

"Ogden Specialty Woods, 15 Durham Street, Stockport," read John. "Are they open on weekends?"

Mr. Hume rubbed his forehead, which is what he did when he was thinking, and said ,"I believe so. I remember going there on a Saturday."

Conan had football practice (for which he was already late), so John and Alex ran to the Cunningham home as fast as Alex could go, which really wasn't all that fast. They threw down their schoolbags, rushed past Miriam, who was watching television, and went into the kitchen where the telephone was. Katie had spread her schoolwork over much of the table and scowled when they came in to disrupt her peaceful study.

"Don't mess up my schoolwork!" she demanded bossily.

"Alex, do you have the card Mr. Hume gave us?" asked John, ignoring Katie.

"No!" I gave it to you!"

John searched through his pockets and finally ran for his school bag. Fortunately the card was tucked into his notebook.

"Quick," said Alex, "dial it before they can close for the day."

"Don't make so much noise," complained Katie. "You're pushing my papers around."

John dialed the number. It rang several times, making John think they must already be closed. But at last someone picked up the line.

"Ogden Specialty Woods," said a woman in a thin, high voice.

"I'm looking for an ash pole, two inches…."

"Just a minute, I'll connect you to Sales," she said. There was a click and then music on the line.

"Hello, this is Jeffrey," said Jeffrey in a quick, businesslike voice.

"Hello, Mr. Jeffrey. My name is John. I'm working on a school project. I need a pole made of ash. Two inches in diameter and seven feet long." The part about this being a school project was stretching the truth a bit, but as Mr. Hume was helping them, it was probably okay, he thought.

"School project, huh? What school is that?"

"Allerton Primary School, in Wythenshawe."

"I see. Well, ash doesn't normally come in poles. We cut all our ash in one-inch thick boards. It's used for fine furniture."

"Uh, we've looked everywhere. Our teacher, Mr. Hume, says he buys wood from you and thought you might have something."

"Jack Hume?"

"Yes, I think so."

Jeffrey's tone changed immediately. "I know Jack well. Good chap! Well, we don't have any ash poles, but we've got some uncut ash out back. We do our own sawyering, you know."

"No, I didn't know. What's sawyering?"

Jeffrey laughed. "Jack can tell you all about it. It means we cut our own wood. If you can come down here, we can look through our stock of ash and see what we can do for you."

John put his hand over the mouthpiece and whispered to Alex, who was looking very anxious indeed. "They cut their own wood!" Alex broke into a broad smile and gave him a thumbs-up.

"I'll have to talk with my Dad to see when we can come. Are you open on Saturdays?"

"Yes. Just ask for Jeffrey. What kind of project is this?"

John hesitated. Alex stopped smiling because of the look on John's face. John decided on the truth, at least part of it.

64

"Well, we're working with Mr. Hume...uh...to build a replica of a broomstick we saw in an old book. Sort of a project."

"Why ash, then? I can get you pine poles all the day long."

"Uh, the instructions say ash. It has to be two inches thick and relatively straight, and there can't be any bark on it at all."

"Interesting. I'll have to give Jack a call. Very curious. Well, come on down any Saturday and ask for me. We close at three o'clock on Saturdays, mind you."

John said "thank you" and hung up. He borrowed Alex's pencil to write "Jeffrey" on the back of the business card. And, just out of curiosity, he used a kitchen chair to reach to the top of the refrigerator, pulled down the telephone book, and looked under "lumber yards." Sure enough, Ogden Specialty Woods was listed there, in tiny print.

"We wouldn't have gotten to the O's for another month," said Alex.

"And I don't think Jeffrey would've helped us if I hadn't mentioned Mr. Hume."

Chapter 23

Mum and Dad didn't make John do his homework on Fridays, although he did have to put some time in every Saturday. Usually John watched television on Friday evenings. Once in a while, Dad, Mum, Katie, John, and Miriam would go to a restaurant or a pub for a night out—they didn't usually go to the Clap Hammer Pub because Mum didn't think much of their menu and thought the place was too noisy. John liked it when they went to hamburger restaurants, because he thought fancy food tasted, well, fancy, and he didn't like it. And anyway, Miriam usually wanted chips with everything she ordered, and fancy restaurants often didn't have chips.

Conan went to the movies with his mum and Alex was at home with an upset stomach. Television offered only reruns, and anyway, John was drawn to the handwritten book.

He went into his bedroom. He never really thought of it this way, but his bedroom was rather tiny. Inside he had a bed, of course, because no bedroom is complete without a bed. The bed had once belonged to his uncle, who had used it before he got married. It had a simple iron bedstead, with bronze bars in loops and swirls. John actually was rather proud of this. The corners of the bedstead stuck up so that he could hang things there, like a cap or his sweater, though his mum told him that hanging a sweater like that would stretch it out of shape.

He had four more pieces of furniture in his bedroom.

He had his grandfather's dresser, which was really too large for the room, but it just fit on the wall opposite the bed and next to the door. The old oak dresser had five drawers, each with two round knobs. He'd never used the top drawer, because it had always been too far off the ground for him, so his mum had some old clothes in there that she never wore but said she didn't want to give to charity. The next-to-top drawer was full of John's old clothes—the ones that didn't quite fit anymore. It was the middle drawer that he kept most of his clothes. The drawer below that held John's school clothes. He had three trousers, three sweaters, two ties, and several sets of socks that were for school only. And in the bottom drawer he kept his treasures— little souvenirs of trips and some photographs that Mum let him take with her camera. He was hoping he could get his own camera someday.

The next piece of furniture was an old wardrobe, which Mum and Dad never talked much about, so John suspected it came from a yard sale somewhere. There really wasn't much in it—his good jacket and a raincoat, plus his school shirts. It was mostly empty. John didn't like it much—it looked like it had been set out in the rain once, and the veneer along one side was mottled and warped. The extra set of trainers that John kept in the bottom were really too small. In fact the trainers he wore now were rather small for his feet—John supposed he would have to get around to telling Mum that it was time for a new pair. But he didn't want to, because Mum always sighed when it was time for new trainers. John never wore the old ones out before he needed new ones. Mum said he was growing "so fast," which John took to mean "too fast." But he really wasn't any taller than most of his schoolmates.

The tiny bedside table, about eighteen inches square, stood on spindly legs. The table, painted a pale green, had a single drawer, though not much would fit inside. On the table stood a nice reading lamp and John's rusty alarm clock, which right now read about 7:00 p.m. The table, of course, was placed between the chair and the bed, so John could use the reading lamp whether he was in the chair or in bed.

Dad had picked out the chair at a real furniture store three years earlier, saying John needed a nice place to read. It was actually a hard-backed wood chair with two curvy arms and looked like it might belong in an old library. Mum found a pad for the seat. John liked this chair.

It was on this that John sat after pulling the handwritten book out from under his mattress.

Chapter 24

John opened to the section on Cartomancy on Page 26. Cartomancy, John knew from having looked it up on the Internet on the computer at school, is a way to tell fortunes by using cards. Sometimes special cards are used and sometimes a normal deck of playing cards is used. John never played any card games, though he thought he had a deck of cards in his bottom dresser drawer.

Miriam Stoney started the section with a little of her life story.

I was introduced to cartomancy soon after I joined the circus.

Madam Maxine, the woman who would become my mentor in so many

things having to do with magic, tried hard to teach me the rules. I

wrote them down and studied my notes, but it all seemed so confusing!

The trick, I finally discovered, is simple.

The magic comes in two ways. First, the cards must be shuffled in

the presence of the person whose fortune is being told. In fact, the best way is to have the person themselves shuffle the cards, but I discovered quickly that many customers felt a great unease doing this. I don't know why. Perhaps they felt the magic in the air. Perhaps they were suspicious. I had one woman in a dainty dress tell me the cards were dirty and she wouldn't touch them! (And her fortune was a dark one, too.) It is quite important to shuffle the cards carefully. If you are not sure they were shuffled right, shuffle them again and again until you are sure you have captured the person's spirit in the cards.

Some people say that the power of magic is in the deck of cards itself. I do not believe this to be so. The magic comes in shuffling the deck in the presence of the person whose fortune is being told. And then the magic comes in how the cards are read.

The next thing to do is to learn how to read the cards. The cards are taken off the deck and placed face up in front of the person who is the object of the fortunetelling. It is important that once the reading starts, the order of the cards is not disturbed. There are two aspects to the reading of the cards, and I will give the rules here, for they are remarkably complicated. First, each card in the deck represents something. But more importantly, the order in which the cards are revealed represents a life sequence for the fortune-seeker. For example, suppose an ace of clubs comes first, representing a great accomplishment. Next comes the four of spades, representing difficult effort. This could be interpreted two ways. First, something wonderful will happen, followed by difficult times. But it can equally well be read that a great accomplishment is close at hand, but will require hard work.

So how to tell the difference? There is something called the spirit of the cards. Each deck of cards is different, and it is easier to always use the same deck, so you can get to know it well. I recommend that you purchase high-quality playing cards that will last a long time, because if you have to replace them, you must learn the spirit of the new cards and the quality of your fortunes will suffer in the meantime.

I remember one time telling the fortune of a well-dressed young man. I told him that love was about to smile upon him, but that he had competition and needed to be more forthright in courting his intended. He exclaimed that he was indeed interested in two potential companions, but he could not make up his mind which to pursue. The fourth card held the answer—he was to pursue the younger of the two, whom I thought was probably the more beautiful. I cautioned him that she was probably not as well-to-do as the other, but that love with less money was preferable to an uncomfortable but rich existence. He jumped up, said "By Jove, you're right! I know what to do now!" and thanked me profusely. He saw me again a year later when our circus came round again, and told me he was quite happily married. Such events make me feel as though my special calling is very much worthwhile.

But there are times when things do not work out. Some people have personalities that block the spirit of the cards. When I was young, I would persist in telling a fortune, sometimes resulting in being told off! Madam Maxine would console me, because these terrible encounters affected me deeply and sometimes my resulting funk was such that I could not tell fortunes for days at a time. Finally, I learned to recognize this ugly spirit as soon as the person was seated in front of me. I would explain politely that I was unable to tell their fortune, and hoped that their future would be a happy one. I don't have to do this often, but at least once a week someone comes to me who is like this! Once in a while, the person is quite insistent—for this I ask for help from someone else from the circus to explain that I simply cannot tell their fortune at this time—perhaps they can come back later.

Miriam listed rules for interpreting the cards. They went on for pages and pages and pages! John wasn't sure he liked this, so he closed the book and put it back under the mattress.

Chapter 25

Dad didn't have a free day until the second Saturday in December. Alex was too excited to wait until morning to come over, and so he pestered John about a sleepover until Mum gave in. Conan took a far more practical approach. "We aren't leaving until ten o'clock," he pointed out, deciding to sleep in his own bed. But that didn't stop him from showing up for breakfast at 9:00 a.m.

The weather was ghastly. Conan ran in the door, nearly drenched from having run from his house next door. Rain came down in great sheets, splattering and splashing and making puddles even where there were normally no puddles. The wind howled so much they could hear it inside the house.

This time it would be just the boys and Dad in the car, so Alex wouldn't have to sit in the middle seat. The boys ran to the car, but Dad was fussing with the front door, so the boys jumped and hollered until Dad finally had the front door closed and could come out to unlock the car. John took the passenger seat to Dad's left, Conan climbed in behind Dad, and Alex finally, finally got a window seat, but the window promptly fogged up when he breathed on it.

The drive to Stockport should not have taken very long, since Stockport is just to the southeast of Manchester. But the weather caused traffic to slow to a crawl. The windshield wipers on the old Jaguar barely kept up and the rain drummed on the roof so loudly it was hard to hold a conversation. The A-road that led directly to Stockport was crowded, so much so that Dad was thinking of finding an alternate route, but finally they got past where the road was torn up for construction. And they passed three accidents along the way, but none looked serious.

Dad was a bit grumpy that they'd chosen that particular day, but even he admitted it was the only day he had free. The rain showed no sign of letup as they drove through the streets of Stockport. Dad consulted his map frequently.

"Should be about there," he said as they went straight across yet another roundabout. The inside of the car was lit up by a nearby lightning flash. They heard the thunderclap even above the traffic noise. Alex jumped and Conan swore softly.

"Now, now," said Dad.

"Sorry," muttered Conan.

The storm was still in full fury as they drove into the Ogden Specialty Lumber parking lot. The only parking spaces left seemed to be slightly flooded, so Dad took the one that seemed to have the least water in it.

"We'll have to make a run for it. I don't think the storm is going to let up."

John tentatively opened his door. The wind nearly pulled it out of his hand. Taking a deep breath, he dove into the storm, his shoes sinking a good inch into the water. Conan went next, with Alex third. They lost track of Dad as they splashed their way into the door, each of them holding their jackets over their heads in a vain attempt to shield their faces from the rain. Conan got to the big double doors first, yanked them open, and ran in. John held the door open for Alex and Dad.

John shivered and looked around, not liking the feel of soggy socks inside his wet trainers. The first thing that hit him was the smell, a combination of freshly cut wood and an oily something he couldn't define. The place had an enormously high ceiling, like a warehouse, and the rear was lined from top to bottom with lumber in all shapes and varieties. The vast hall echoed from a combination of customers talking and pushing carts around the hardware aisles, the bloop of the scanners at the checkout counters, and, somewhere in a distant corner, a power saw cutting into wood. And still, even though they were inside, they could hear the waves of rain on the warehouse roof and the howl of the wind. John thought it was very noisy. It would not at all be a good place to do homework. At least it was warm inside, if a bit muggy.

This was not at all what John had envisioned. He thought they'd be pulling into some small shop where there was a bear of a man named Jeffrey in an enormous apron who maybe had one apprentice. John wasn't at all prepared for a large store with dozens of employees. Aisle after aisle stretched before them, busy mostly with middle-aged men, but here and there was a middle-aged woman. There were no children or youth anywhere.

"Uh, Dad, what do we do now? How do we find an ash pole?"

"Let's ask for this Jeffrey fellow," said Dad. He led them to a Customer Service Desk in the paint department where they had to wait behind a man who wanted to know what kind of carpenter's glue to use because his seams were always coming loose. Then there was a woman who wanted to know if they carried door hardware. She was directed to Aisle 5 and told there would be a salesman there to help her.

"Yes, sir. How may I help you," said the youngish man with longish hair, wearing a forest-green apron and looking as though he needed a break. He had a pencil behind one ear.

"These boys have a question," said Dad.

"We need an ash pole for a school project," began John, but the youngish man was already shaking his head.

"Don't have ash poles. I've got a few in oak, over there at the end of Aisle 1," he said, pointing.

"But we talked with someone named Jeffrey on the phone," piped up Alex.

"Yes," confirmed John. "He said he might be able to cut something for us."

"Oh. That's Mr. Ogden, the owner. Let me ring him for you."

"Marco alert!" whispered Conan very urgently.

"Where?" exclaimed John. "How'd he find us here?"

"Are you sure, Conan?" said Dad, disbelievingly, staring where Conan was pointing.

"I saw his face. He seemed really surprised to see us, then he looked away. I'm sure it was him!"

Alex hid behind John. "I don't want to have anything to do with him. I thought we were rid of him," he said, sounding scared.

"Jeffrey to Customer Service, please!" boomed the loudspeaker. "Some boys looking for an ash pole."

"Oh, no," muttered John, looking up at Dad. "Now Marco knows what kind of pole we need."

73

"How'd he find us?" muttered Conan.

"Who's that? Who found you?" inquired the youngish man.

"That man down there looking at garden tools who keeps glancing back at us. He's been stalking us."

"Oh, not at all!" chuckled the youngish man. "He's in here every Saturday. Always looking for poles. Odd, really. We've sold him poles made of just about every kind of wood. Oak. Pine. Cherry. Yew. Everything except ash. He's never asked for ash. I remember him because he always complains about the price. Some of the poles he buys are made of very expensive wood. Why, just last week he…."

But they didn't find out what Marco did last week, because he was interrupted by the arrival of Jeffrey Ogden, who turned out to be a bear of a man in a very large forest-green apron, with thick leather gloves stuffed in one pocket and several pens sticking out of the other.

"You must be John!" he boomed, cuffing John on the shoulder. "And you with the ponytail, that'd be Conan, right? And that leaves Alex. Must be you," he said, addressing himself to Alex.

"Uh, how'd you know our names, sir?" ventured John, using his most polite voice because Dad was standing right behind him.

"I called Jack right after you called me. Jack's been a customer of ours for many years," enthused Ogden. "In fact, I've told him many times if he ever gets tired of teaching, I'll give him a job here. There isn't much about wood he doesn't know! He's done work for me, moonlighting."

"Did he tell you about our project?" asked John, feeling unaccountably nervous about being greeted so loudly. He glanced over his shoulder at Marco, who sneaked a peak in their direction and then went back to examining gardening tools. This time he picked up a rake and pretended to check it for true. John thought he must have an interesting patch of grass that would need raking in a December storm.

"Oh, yes! A broomstick, huh! Well, I might be able to help you. Come with me into the back. I have a piece of ash that just might fill the bill."

And without waiting, he set off toward the back of the store, in the direction where all the lumber was stacked. John walked very quickly to keep up with him and Alex had to run. Ogden led them down the paint aisle. "We got every wood paint and stain known to mankind," he said. They went through a double door at the back of the giant room into another room that was not as big but was still large.

The first thing John noticed was that it was cold here. He soon saw why. In reality, they were in a large shed and the very back of the shed was completely open to the weather. He heard the rain pounding on the metal shed roof and saw water pouring off and splattering on the ground all along the shed opening.

The next thing John noticed were the tree trunks. Pieces of tree trunk, that is. Most were thick, cut eight or ten feet long, others thin. Some were sawed in half, others were intact. He could tell that many different kinds of trees were represented here, but he would have been hard-pressed to name even one of them.

The third thing John noticed were the saws. Some of them were the strangest contraptions John had ever seen—huge tables with giant saw blades that seemed as tall as he was. None of the giant tools were in use. John assumed it was because it was Saturday.

"We buy cut wood, of course, but we're the only specialty sawyer in the North of England with this kind of equipment. Why, I've got yew and seventeen varieties of oak, and look—this just in—an ash tree that's been standing dead for ten years behind a derelict barn—got it for a bargain price! The wood's completely dry. Couldn't ask for better!" He had led them to what looked like an enormously thick tree trunk, bigger around than John, Conan and Alex could reach if they held hands and tried to surround it.

"Uh," stammered John, trying to be heard above the clatter of the rainfall. "We just need a two inch pole. The book says it can be thicker, though. It says it should come from a branch."

"Look right here," boomed Ogden above the storm. He reached behind the trunk and pulled out a branch. "Didn't know what we were going to do with it, to tell you the truth—one of

75

my boys threw it on the truck by mistake. Too thin to make lumber from, but it would sure make good firewood. About eight feet long and relatively straight. Yes, I think we can make your broomstick pole from this." He looked as though he were expecting applause.

But John was flummoxed.

Conan jumped in. "How do we make a pole out of a branch?" he asked. "The branch looks too big. And we can't have any bark."

"You didn't see my tools, did you? I'll show you. Like I said, it's the best set of saws in the North of England for this kind of work. We're not a lumber mill, but for specialty lumber, there's none better!"

He picked up the branch as though it were a toothpick. John's mouth hung open. Dad made a feeble move as though to help him, but Ogden seemed to have matters well in hand. He carefully placed the log onto a table saw that had a blade that seemed to be two feet in diameter. He bustled with the equipment.

"Gotta fasten it down good. Then we'll zip away at it and cut it down to size. I think maybe you'd be better with a pole about two and a half inches in diameter. More strength, if it's going to hold the three of you." He winked.

"I guess so," stammered John, but his response was lost in the wind noise.

"Stand back," commanded Ogden. "Put on some goggles." He handed around four sets of goggles and took one for himself.

A moment later John, Conan, Alex and Dad put their fingers in their ears as the giant blade began to whir. A second later and it was screaming as it sliced the edge off the branch. After a few more adjustments and more screaming, Ogden was holding up a two-and-a-half-inch square pole about eight feet long with ragged ends. John was amazed how quickly it had happened.

"Now we have to turn it," said Ogden.

"Turn it?" asked Alex. "Which way?"

"No, Alex. On a lathe. Follow me."

And so they did, going over to another enormous contraption that looked like the giant-sized version of what Mr. Hume had in

76

the school basement. In a moment, Ogden had the square pole secured in place.

"Ash is mighty hard wood, so I'm going to do this in two stages. You can stay to watch if you want, but it'll take about an hour."

"Boys, why don't we have some lunch and let Mr. Ogden tend to his other customers while the lathe does its work," suggested Dad.

"Mr. Ogden," said the youngish man who appeared out of nowhere and made John jump. "The man who's always buying poles is out here again. This time he wants an ash pole."

"Him?" said Mr. Ogden. "The bloke who never wants to pay what it's worth? Tell him I've got just enough stock to make one for these boys, but he'll have to wait until we saw the big block." He waved at the massive tree trunk, just missing Alex, who ducked. "We've got lots of ash in stock up front, so we may not be sawing it for a month or so." He considered for a moment. "Tell him it'll be about a hundred and twenty quid, too. Maybe that'll put him off. Crazy bloke."

John's stomach was suddenly in knots. "A hundred and twenty quid!" He stared at Alex and then at Dad. "Mr. Ogden, we don't have that much money!"

Mr. Ogden smiled indulgently at the boys as the youngish man set off for the main warehouse.

"I'm not going to charge you a hundred and twenty pounds. I'm doing this as a favor for Jack Hume. You should see the cherrywood dresser he made for me! He didn't charge me but a quarter of what it was worth. How about five pounds? Can you afford that?"

John couldn't.

He stared at Alex and Conan, who stared back. Never at any point had they considered that the broomstick materials might cost them something.

"Mr. Ogden," said Dad, "you're being more than kind. I think I can handle that on behalf of the boys."

John, Conan, and Alex were very relieved.

Chapter 26

The three boys and Dad were in a noisy, crowded hamburger restaurant in Stockport, arguing about Marco.

"He must know something about what's in the handwritten book, if he's out looking for poles," said Conan.

"But he didn't know it was ash," pointed out Alex.

"Why's he trying to make a flying broomstick anyway?" mused John.

"Because the old lady said she saw us flying on a broomstick. I'll bet he's trying to beat us to it!" stated Alex, taking a bite of his hamburger for emphasis.

"What I don't get is how he knew to find us here," puzzled Dad, poking a chip into some ketchup.

"According to the guy in the store, he's there every Saturday," said John, removing another pickle from his hamburger. "I should've ordered it without pickles." He added the pickle to the little pile on his napkin.

"But how would he know to go to that particular store?" asked Alex, picking up one of John's pickles without asking and tossing it into his mouth.

"If Mr. Ogden is right, it's the only place around here for exotic woods," said Dad, putting down his hamburger and looking out at the driving rain.

"Marco now knows the handle has to be ash," said John. "I'll bet he's built several broomsticks. That must mean he knows where Castle Alox is!"

"Maybe he doesn't know," said Alex, sneaking another pickle and stuffing it into the remains of his hamburger before taking another bite. "Maybe he's going to shadow us to find out."

"I hope not," said Conan, shivering slightly at the thought.

The three boys and Dad dashed to the old Jaguar through the sheets of rain. Alex tripped and fell headlong in the parking lot, soaking his jeans. He was instantly on his feet and sought the refuge of the back seat, slamming the door behind him. They made their way through the flooded streets back to Ogden Specialty Woods in the never-ending rain.

Once they ran inside, they went up to the Customer Service Desk. The youngish man was there.

"Oh, I'm glad you came back. Was worried about you. We had the pole up front, but that old man tried to run off with it, so I've got it in the back. Let me get it for you."

The boys exchanged meaningful glances. Conan's head swiveled like a radar antenna, but Marco was not in sight. The youngish man came back with the pole, now trimmed to seven feet long and smelling of newly-cut wood.

"Let me put it in plastic for you against the rain," said the youngish man, which he did. "Nasty day out! Here's your ticket —you can pay at the counter."

"Thank you," said John, using his politest voice.

"Please thank Mr. Ogden for us, will you?" said Dad.

"Did that old man order an ash pole?" asked Conan eagerly.

The youngish man scratched his ear. "Yes, in fact he did. At least he tried. But Ogden wouldn't take the order until he put down half the money, so he left about a half hour ago. Strange bloke. But he'll be back when he raises the money, no doubt." He smiled and scratched his ear again.

Dad paid the £5 for the pole after the four of them stood in line for a long time. Saturday must be their busy day, thought John. They made sure the plastic was wrapped very tightly around the pole and went into the storm, with John carrying the pole. It seemed oddly heavy, perhaps because it was extra hard wood, John thought. It made the journey to the car seem long.

And the pole barely fit into the car, stretching between John and Dad in front all the way to the back window.

Chapter 27

On Monday morning, Dad walked with them to school after many requests from the boys.

"What if Marco is waiting for us?" said John, passing the bread to Katie during Sunday dinner at the round kitchen table.

"Yeah! What if he tries to steal the pole!" piped up Alex, helping himself to seconds.

"He's bigger than we are!" claimed Conan. "I bet I can outrun him, though."

"We don't want him to get it!" said John, putting his fork down. "You've simply *got* to guard us when we go to school!"

And so Dad called into his work and said he'd be a little late because of a 'special errand.'

There was no sign of Marco on the way to school. Fortunately, the storm had blown itself out and a watery sunlight shone down on them. It was cold and there was enough of a breeze to make their cheeks sting.

"You scared him away, Mr. Cunningham," said Alex as they stood at the Allerton's front gate, a good fifteen minutes before they'd normally get there.

"I'll bet he didn't want to take four of us on," commented Conan. "He's afraid to show his face again."

"Thanks, Dad," said John simply.

John held the pole up so he wouldn't bang on any of the other students. "We've got to find Mr. Hume."

They had an anxious ten minutes looking for Mr. Hume, finally finding him by knocking on the staff room door. Mr. Hume took the pole from them without a word and the boys ran to line up for their first classes.

That afternoon, Mr. Hume told them they couldn't possibly make a broomstick out of such a fine piece of wood until they treated it properly. "It'll get wet and warp! It needs to be sanded and properly varnished!"

Conan had to go to football practice, so he changed into his football gear and went onto the wet fields with some reluctance, not really wanting to be completely muddy and bone cold for the next hour.

John and Alex stayed in the crafts room, where each put on an apron and was handed several sheets of sandpaper. They set to work. They sanded for what seemed like hours to them and only thirty minutes according to the wall clock. Finally Mr. Hume told them they could stop. He showed them how to use a tack cloth to clean the wood and then sand some more. When it was time to go, he said they'd sand again the next day, which is exactly what they did, though Conan was available to help them this time.

Mr. Hume had them apply a thin coat of varnish, which would set overnight. On Wednesday, the boys sanded this again, though Conan was absent for football practice. They were beginning to hate sandpaper and all the dust it created, especially since it showed easily on their navy blue uniform pants. And then they laid another coat of varnish over this. On Thursday, they used very fine sandpaper on Wednesday's varnish and then varnished again, this time with a different varnish. It looked very shiny. On Friday, they repeated this, using yet another type of varnish which smelled oily and stinky.

"I'll bet Conan's glad he's at football practice and he's missing this," said Alex as he brushed on the varnish and wrinkled his nose.

"How are you boys doing finding your twigs?" asked Mr. Hume, who seemed to be enjoying the smell. "Looks like you're almost done with the pole."

"Twigs?" asked John and Alex at the same time. "What twigs?"

"For the broom part of the broom," said Mr. Hume, his eyes twinkling. He rubbed his palms together. "Takes more than a pole to make a broom, you know."

Chapter 28

John, Conan and Alex were at a bit of a loss after school as they gathered at the round kitchen table in the Cunningham's home. John threw his school bag in his room and retrieved the handwritten book to see what it had to say.

"Katie, turn down the telly!" yelled John as he went through the living room on the way into the kitchen.

"I can't hear it with you guys making such a racket in the kitchen!" yelled Katie back.

Miriam reached up to turn down the television, but only a little.

"Miriam, don't do what he says," said Katie. "He's bossing us around!"

"I am not!" insisted John, who went into the kitchen and pulled the door shut behind him. He reckoned that if his parents had been home, the television would never be permitted to be this loud.

"Stupid sister," muttered John under his breath as he plopped the handwritten book on the table.

"So what kinds of twigs are we looking for?" asked Alex, throwing his school bag in a corner.

"Why can't we just use a couple real brooms and get straw that way?" asked Conan.

"Let's see what the old lady said in the book," insisted John. "We have to do it the right way."

And so they reread the section in the handwritten book that described how to construct a flying broomstick. As it turned out, Miriam Stoney wrote even more on the twigs than she did on the ash handle.

It is the twigs attached to the broomstick pole that give it its true magic. Both the birch and the willow yield twigs that have long been known to be useful in many ways, some of them now exploited commercially.

For example, the willow's bark yields medicines which have been used for centuries. Chewing on the bark can yield relief from pain and many ailments. And the birch is even more useful, as it can be combined in potions which yield most excellent results. The birch is also used for flavorings in some potions to make them more palatable, and the sap of the birch can be drunk. But one must beware the birch, for it can make one sneeze. Birch also makes excellent firewood, though that is not our purpose here, for what is useful for the flying broomstick is the twig.

The twigs should be gathered in the morning and should be freshly-dropped from the tree by natural means. Never should twigs be pulled from a tree, for this separates them from their life source prematurely and this negative influence will make the broomstick fly less well. Also, it is best not to use twigs that have been on the ground for too long, as the natural decay processes will have begun. One good time to collect twigs is after a storm, for a storm is a natural event, therefore any twigs on the ground will still be healthy and full of life force, yet will have been separated naturally.

Be sure to gather an ample supply of twigs, and apply them in the correct ratio as shown in the chart. If desired, for effect, it is possible to mix in broom straw, as is used today in the making of brooms for sale, but it should be remembered that broom straw added merely for decoration has no effect whatsoever on the broom's flying ability and therefore the effort is largely wasted. I have seen broom straw that has been dyed added to a broom to add some flash and color, but I personally do not recommend it, as I think the addition was done as a replacement for some of the willow and birch twigs, being deleterious to the magic of the broom.

"What's 'deleterious'?" asked Alex, looking at John, puzzled.

"It means 'bad,'" replied Conan.

"Why didn't she just say 'bad'?" asked Alex, looking annoyed. They continued reading.

The twigs should be eighteen to twenty inches long and selected with as few bends as possible. After collection, they should be soaked overnight in a solution of water and alum, a substance known to the ancients for its magical properties. Then the twigs should be thoroughly dried before fastening to the broom pole.

"What's alum?" asked Alex, once again puzzled.

"No idea," said Conan. "Probably dangerous."

"I think we used it in science class last year. We'll have to ask Mr. Hume," said John, closing the book. "The big problem now is finding a birch tree and a willow tree."

"I don't know what either looks like," said Alex, shaking his head.

"A willow tree is all loopy and hangs down. I think there's one on the school grounds," offered Conan.

And so the next day they asked their science teacher, Ms. Bryant, about birch and willow trees. When asked why, John told her that it was for a project they were doing with Mr. Hume. "That's odd," she said. "I never heard of that project. But there's a nice willow out back. No leaves on it in January, of course. But you can check. It's rather sloppy today—I don't think the children are allowed onto the field just now—too wet. But in a few days."

"What about a birch tree?" asked Conan, fidgeting with his school bag as though embarrassed.

"I don't know," said Ms. Bryant. "Perhaps you can call the Manchester Parks Department and ask for their botanist."

"What's a botanist?" asked Alex.

"They know all about plants," said Conan.

84

"That's right," said Ms. Bryant. "But it's almost time for my next class. You'd best run along so you're not late."

Chapter 29

The football scrimmage scheduled for that afternoon was called on account of an unplayable field, so the boys went to see Mr. Hume, who was busy cleaning up after a second year art class. It was cold in his room.

"How are you coming on your twig hunt?" he asked, smiling at them.

"What's alum?" asked Alex, looking curious and putting his school bag up on a desk.

"A chemical," replied Mr. Hume. "Why?"

"We have to soak the twigs overnight in water and alum," replied John, watching Mr. Hume closely to see if he showed any signs of shock or dismay, but there were none.

"Pretty common chemical," he said. "I think we can find some. I use it sometimes in preparing things for crafts." He smiled, picking up a small bucket full of paint brushes the second years had just used. "Soak the twigs overnight, huh? That means you've got to find them, first. Any luck?"

"Ms. Bryant says there's a willow in the back of the schoolyard," replied Conan. "But we don't know what to do about a birch."

Mr. Hume looked thoughtful. "There's a lovely birch in a park not far from where I live. But the parks people keep things pretty clean. Not sure if they'd let you boys just cut twigs."

"We can't cut them," replied John. "They have to be new fallen. The book says specifically not to cut the twigs."

Mr. Hume sat down and began pulling brushes out of the bucket, sorting them by size to be put away for their next use. Each looked well-used.

"What about Wythenshawe Park?" he asked. "They have a Horticultural Centre there. Haven't you boys been there?"

"Just in the summertime," replied Conan. "They have concerts and things. Mum and I used to go there a lot, sometimes with Dad...." His voice trailed off.

"Is that the park that has the barnyard?" asked Alex, who picked up one of the brushes that Mr. Hume had put into the wrong pile. He put it into the right pile.

"That's the one. Should be lots of birch trees there."

And so Mr. Hume helped John look up the telephone number for the Horticulture Centre at Wythenshawe Park. John had to call the number three times before anyone answered. When someone finally did, they told John that not much happened in the winter there—the plants were asleep. At least he didn't ask what sort of school project it was, and agreed to let John, Conan and Alex gather as many twigs as they wanted to the following Saturday. "There's a storm blowing in Friday, so I 'spect there'll be plenty for ya," he said. "In fact, if you'd take them all, you'd be doing me a favor!" John replied they just needed enough for the school project, maybe an armful each of birch and willow.

And on the last Saturday of January, that's what they did. The storm on Friday was very windy—so much so it howled all night. But Saturday dawned clear and very cold, so John, Conan and Alex bundled up in their warmest clothes, complete with boots, scarves and gloves. Dad took along several large black trash bags so they'd have something to put the twigs in.

They drove to the park in silence. They had a little trouble finding the person that John had talked with, mostly because John hadn't written down his name and had since forgotten it—it turned out to be Dennis. Dennis led them through the frigid pathways to the Horticultural Centre, pointing out different kinds of trees and shrubs. Most, he said, looked much better in the summer.

At last he led them to a birch tree. "Lovely specimen," he proclaimed, "though it could do with some leaves." A fairly strong specimen, too, since not all that many twigs had dropped. John and Alex gathered what they could while Conan held his arms in front of him like a front loader, into which the twigs were piled. "Not that one," said Conan every time Alex tried to add a short one to the pile. Or sometimes he'd say "too many bends." At last they decided they had enough. Dad helped John and Alex fit a big plastic trash bag over the twigs while Conan tried to hold them still.

Dennis had four varieties of willow tree for them to look at. They finally decided to take some twigs from each, just in case. They quit when Conan had his arms full.

Chapter 30

On the last Monday in January, John, Conan and Alex fought their way home clutching their cloaks tightly about them. The chill wind howled and moaned and made the trees on Brixton Street creak even though they didn't have any leaves; they still flapped their branches in protest.

None of the boys spoke on the way home. When Alex tried to shout something, it was lost in the wind. Automatically, the boys headed to the Cunningham home because both Conan's and Alex's homes would be dark. Their hope was that Katie and Miriam were already home, because the boys had stayed behind at school with Mr. Hume. He'd located two large vats that looked like washing tubs. They took these down into the forbidden basement and filled them with water. The handwritten book hadn't said how much alum to use, so they divided the little bag of alum evenly between the two vats. The biggest problem they had was that the twigs wanted to float. Finally Mr. Hume solved the problem by putting odd-shaped wood scraps on top of the twigs, thus forcing the twigs under the surface, if only by a little bit.

John struggled with his door key while Conan and Alex jumped up and down to stay warm. Finally Katie opened the door for them because John couldn't get his key to work. The boys rushed inside and slammed the door shut behind them. They went into the kitchen, which always seemed the warmest room in the house during the winter, and found Katie and Miriam at the round table doing their homework.

"A letter came for you today," said Miriam, holding it up.

"Who would write to me?" asked John, taking the envelope. "There's no return address."

The envelope was certainly battered. There was a coffee stain on the back—a round, brown ring. And the front was addressed to John Cunningham, 14 Brixton Street, Wythenshawe, Manchester. The handwriting looked a little like Aunt Emma's, with old-fashioned loopiness and a little bit of jitter here and there.

Alex took the letter and bent it back and forth as though to see if it would break in half. "It looks like an old man's handwriting," he pronounced confidently.

"How can you tell?" asked Conan, taking the letter from Alex and holding it up to the light.

"It looks like my grandfather's," replied Alex.

"Let's open it," said John, taking it from Conan. "I haven't gotten a letter just for me since Aunt Emma sent me a birthday card last summer."

John pulled the flap open and pulled out a single sheet of three-hole notebook paper. The holes had been ripped out like someone had grabbed the sheet of paper and simply ripped it from the notebook without bothering to open the three-ring binder properly. Conan and Alex crowded next to John so they could look over his shoulders. There was no date on the letter.

John,
You and your buddies are playing a dangerous game keeping the book. It will kill you! My wife should not have given you the book because it is mine and I want it back! I think you were lying when you said you can open it, and even if you have you should understand that its contents will lead you to certain death. I MUST have that book back, and if you do not return it, you must face the consequences, and I shall ensure they come swiftly. I tried to offer you money for it, but you foolishly would not take it, so now I will resort to other measures. Take the book to the Clap Hammer Pub and give it to the barman.

He'll know what to do with it. If you have already figured out how to open it, LEAVE IT OPEN, or I shall have to take additional retaliatory steps. Do not try to trace me, for that is impossible.   Marco

Chapter 31

"How did he know my name?" asked John, astonished. He looked on the reverse side, but there was nothing. He turned the envelope upside down to see if there was anything else inside, but it was empty.

"What are we going to do?" asked Alex, apprehensively. "How did he find us, anyway?"

"What does he mean, 'retaliatory?' What could he do to us?" asked Conan, though he sounded skeptical instead of scared.

"What's going on," asked Katie. "Are you boys in trouble again?"

"Let's make sure the book is safe!" said John, so the boys thundered down the hallway with Katie's protests ringing in their ears, but they ignored her.

John jumped on his bed and fairly tore it apart to get at the book, but it was safe and sound under the mattress near the wall. He pulled the book out and sat on the edge of his bed. Conan sat on one side and Alex on the other, while John opened the book and glanced through its pages.

"It's safe," he said. "It looks all right."

"So what do we do now," asked Conan, shifting slightly. "Can I see the letter again?"

John handed him the letter, now folded back in the envelope.

Conan pulled out the letter. "It says we're to leave it with the barman at the Clap Hammer. Do you think Marco is hiding there?"

"So close to us?" asked John incredulously. He took the envelope back. "The postmark is Leeds. It was sent on Saturday."

"That's not very far away," said Alex, laying back on John's bed with his feet dangling on the floor.

"So the barman must be someone who knows him. Maybe we could go down to the Clap Hammer and ask the barman about this?" suggested Conan, who likewise lay back on John's bed.

John got up to pace the small room. "It's about 4:30," he said, glancing at his alarm clock. "It's already dark. And the weather's horrible. I think we should have Dad go with us when we go down there. What if Marco is already about? He might chase us back here and force us to give him the book."

"He's got to be with the circus, wherever they go in the winter," said Conan reasonably, sitting up. "But don't we need to tell the barman that we're not going to give up the book?"

"What's deadly about the old book," said Alex, hefting the book and sniffing it.

"It's what's written in the book," assured John. "Not the book itself."

"But the book itself is magic. We know that," insisted Alex, gingerly putting the book on John's chair.

"We've had it for several months now and nothing's happened to any of us," said John reasonably, picking up the book. "We haven't tried any of the potions, yet."

Alex shuddered. "This is spooky. Why does Marco want the book? Can't he ask the old woman anytime?"

"He says in the letter that the old woman is his wife. Yet she says in the book that he's her brother. Very fishy."

"When does your Dad come home?"

"Usually about six o'clock."

And so the boys decided the best thing to do was attempt their homework, so they joined Katie and Miriam at the round table in the kitchen. But they kept talking about the book, and Katie kept telling them to be quiet, and the result was that nobody got much homework done by the time Dad and Mum came home. The boys rushed to meet them at the door, which John was able to open before Dad could make his key work.

"Mr. Cunningham, you should see the letter!" yelled Alex.

"Dad, I just got the strangest letter!" yelled John at the same time.

"Wait! Hold on there a minute. Let us get inside and take our coats off. Keep your ears on."

"You better look at this letter," said Conan, but Dad first helped Mum out of her coat and then took his own off while Alex hopped up and down.

"All right," said Dad. "What's this letter."

John thrust it at him. "Just came today," he said.

Dad's face became grim. "Let me see the envelope."

"There's no return address," said John. "Postmarked in Leeds on Saturday."

Mum took the letter. Her face was quickly grim, too. "Honey, I think we should call the police."

"I agree," said Dad, who promptly went into the kitchen and headed straight for the telephone. He picked it up and dialed 999.

John, Conan and Alex followed. Katie and Miriam looked up, puzzled by Dad's air of determination.

"No, this is not an emergency. But my son has just received a very threatening letter."

"Yes, I'll wait."

"My 10-year-old son has received a letter with a thinly-veiled death threat."

"Received today."

"No return address. Signed by a fellow named Marco. I've met him. An old man from the circus. We saw him in Buxton. He somehow found us here. His sister gave my son a book, and this fellow's been after it ever since. He's already been stalking my son. We ordered him off."

Dad stood by the refrigerator, one hand idly brushing the sink. He looked as though he was trying to bore holes in the telephone to make the police understand the urgency of the situation. John knew that when Dad turned red it was a good time to be very conciliatory.

"Postmarked Leeds, Saturday."

Dad read them the letter.

"Yes, I know he says wife. But the book says Marco is her brother."

"Yes, I've looked at the book."

"No, we haven't seen him in a couple months. I guess he must've traced the number on the car. But I don't know how he knew our son's name."

"The Clap Hammer is just down the street from us."

"No, I don't frequent it."

"The boys don't want to give up the book. Are you going to look into this or not? My boy is being stalked and now we've received this letter!"

"Very well," said Dad, and hung up.

He turned to the boys, still red in the face. "They said they'll send someone round to take a look at it, but it might be awhile. In the meantime, Alex and Conan, you'd better call your mums."

"Can we stay here?" piped up Alex. "I want to talk with the policeman, too!"

In the end, both boys stayed for dinner, which Mum and Dad worked together to prepare, a casserole that needed to be baked for an hour. Mum was a little cross with Katie, because she was supposed to have preheated the oven before Mum and Dad got home, but Katie protested the boys had been making so much noise that she'd forgotten. In the meantime, Dad, still cross, told the boys to get their homework done, so they tried to do this, but truth be told, they were too excited that a policeman would be coming soon to get much done.

Detective Sergeant Selby rang the doorbell at 8:00 p.m., give or take a few minutes. He looked over the letter very carefully. "I've already been down to the Clap Hammer," he said. "The barman denies knowing anyone named Marco. I gave him my card and asked him to call me if anyone by that name shows up. He's an old man, you say?"

And in spite of everything the boys told him, he brushed aside their concerns. "He wanted the book. Sometimes people get a little funny about family heirlooms. Why don't you just give it back?"

"The old woman said we were to have it!" said Conan fiercely.

"We're keeping it," said Alex.

"Very well then, lads." He looked at his watch. "I have two more calls this evening. Here's my card. Give me a call if this Marco fellow shows up. You know," he said smirking, "if you can get a picture of him, that would help."

And that was all they could get out of him. Dad was still red.

John led the boys down the hallway with all the family pictures. He sat in his chair and Conan and Alex sat on the bed. He had his school notebook with him.

"If the stupid policeman won't help," he said, "we've got to do this on our own."

"But how?" asked Alex.

"We'll go to the Clap Hammer tomorrow and leave a note for Marco."

"By ourselves?" asked Conan.

"I've got it all worked out," said John. He opened his notebook, where he began to write. Alex jumped up to see what he was writing, but Conan waited on the bed.

"'We are not giving the book back. We know you are Miriam's brother, not her husband. Stay away from us. If you come near us, we will take your photo and give it to the police, who have already seen your threatening letter. Signed John.' How's that?"

"Cool," replied Conan.

Chapter 32

After school the next day they carefully removed the twigs from the soaking tubs and laid them out on the vast concrete floor in the forbidden basement.

"I think we have too many twigs," said Conan, eyeing never-ending piles. He'd peeled off his coat and sweater and was down to his light blue school shirt and navy tie.

"That way we can pick the best," assured Mr. Hume. "It's fairly damp down here. But it has good air circulation because of the furnace, plus it stays quite warm. Lucky we have so much room."

"What do we do with all the water in the tubs?" asked Alex, putting down the last of the twigs to dry, which were in mostly neat rows, divided by birch and willow.

"Too heavy to move," said Mr. Hume. "Let me show you something. Help me with this hosepipe."

Under Mr. Hume's direction, they disconnected the hosepipe, which was in the basement to use to wash down the floor into the floor drain. They then gently lowered the hosepipe, one end first, into the tub that had held willow twigs. Mr. Hume made them lower it carefully so that it wound around at the bottom of the tub. Then Mr. Hume put his thumb over the end of the hosepipe and drew it carefully out of the tub and pulled it over by the floor drain and let his thumb go. Water gushed from the end.

"Siphon," he said simply.

"That's like magic," said Alex.

They couldn't get all the water out of the tub with the siphon, so Mr. Hume picked up one handle and Conan took the other. John helped a little but Alex was really more in the way. They pulled and dragged the tub, slopping a little water on the floor, until it was next to the drain. Mr. Hume then carefully tipped the tub up on its side so the water poured down the floor drain. They then repeated the whole process with the other tub. At last, they were finished.

As they bundled up, Mr. Hume told them it would take several days for the twigs to dry. "And don't forget your linen yarn," he said, smiling at them. "Then we can build your magic broomstick."

Chapter 33

It was a little after 4:00 p.m. when they left Allerton Primary School, once again bundled up with scarves and gloves. The raw wind had abated, but it was still very cold, and now, in the late afternoon, it was getting dark.

"Are you sure about this," asked Alex, looking at John from under his huge navy blue scarf.

"Follow me," replied John.

Together they crossed the High Street and turned right, following the High Street, down about a hundred yards to the Clap Hammer Pub. The old sign hanging over the sidewalk announced simply "The Clap Hammer," with the clap hammer from a large bell hanging next to the sign. The boys pushed open the double doors, feeling very out of place in their school clothes. The place was nearly empty. It held about fifteen round tables with four hardback chairs each. Booths lined the walls, which were dimly lit and held framed pictures and advertisements for various brands of whiskey, beer, and other drinks. A large bar sat at the back, brown and imposing, with dozens of empty glasses gleaming in neat rows. From a back room they could hear the clack of snooker balls. Otherwise the place was nearly empty.

"Boys! You're underage! You want me to lose my license?" yelled the barman as the boys let the doors swing shut behind them.

John bravely reached in his schoolbag as the barman came around from behind the bar to shoo them out. He pulled out the envelope with their message. Written on the front was simply 'Marco' with a return address of 'John.' He held it out for the barman to swipe out of his hand.

"Marco!" yelled the barman. "I don't know no Marco. There was a policeman in here yesterday looking for him." He threw the letter back at John. John missed and the letter fell to the floor. Alex picked it up.

"Please, sir, we think he might come calling for it." John took the letter from Alex and thrust it at the barman again.

"The copper said it was about a book, not a letter. There's no book in here."

"We're not giving Marco a book. Please keep this for him," said John.

The barman appraised them long enough for John to feel very uncomfortable. "Why?" he asked at last.

"Just please give it to him if he comes in, okay?"

"The copper said I was to call him if he came in."

"Well, give him this and then call the police."

The barman took the letter. "All right. But mind, I don't know him. What does he look like?"

"Old and creepy," piped Alex, who was hiding behind Conan.

The barman smiled, revealing two missing teeth. "That's most of my customers."

"He'll ask if we brought the book," said John a lot more bravely than he felt. "Just give him this letter."

"Who are you?"

"John. It says so on the envelope."

"John who?"

"Just John. The policeman knows how to find us."

"All right, Just John. But you'd better run along home now. If you want to come into a pub, bring your parents."

They left in a hurry.

Chapter 34

It turned out the linen twine was easy. John and Alex searched the Internet from the school library while Conan was kicking a ball around with some football buddies out on the frozen field.

"Conan sure loves his football," said Alex absentmindedly. "It's freezing outside."

Alex pushed the mouse around while John hovered over his shoulder.

"Not blue," said John. "See if there's any that says 'natural color.' Scroll down."

Alex did so. "Ah. Here's what we want," he said triumphantly.

"Just a minute. Don't do anything! I need to write down the URL so Mum can order it when she goes to work tomorrow."

John scribbled down the shop's URL on his school notebook. The shop was in Reading. He thrust his notebook into his school bag. "Might as well do our homework." He looked out the window. "It's awfully cold out there! Looks like another storm is coming. You can see everyone's breath!"

Alex moved to look out the window too. "Why does Conan like football so much?"

John just shook his head.

Chapter 35

Mum didn't offer too much resistance, seeing as the yarn wasn't that expensive, and placed the order from her computer at work since they didn't have one at home. John offered to place it from a computer in the library, but Mum wasn't about to let them have her bank card number.

The next two weeks were very busy at school, and anyway there was not much to do except wait for the yarn to turn up. Every day after school they worked on their twig pile. Mr. Hume let them into the basement and for the first week they turned over the twigs to make sure they were drying evenly, and then they sorted the twigs to determine which ones they would use. Finally, in mid-February, it was starting to look as though they were dry, plus they had already selected quite a pile of birch and willow twigs that they could use.

Some days they couldn't do anything because Mr. Hume had other things to do. He never let them go down into the forbidden basement without his being there to supervise. He never made a point of it, though. Just a hearty "not today, lads, got a few things to do." He never came right out and said that they couldn't be down there by themselves, but they knew this was the case.

And Conan was falling behind in his schoolwork because of all the football scrimmages he did every day after school. So, on rainy days he would be found in the school library trying to catch up.

On the second Tuesday in February, the boys were crossing the High Street on their way home from school when Conan sucked in his breath. "Look at the pub! Marco!"

John and Conan stopped dead. "Are you sure?" exclaimed Alex.

"Not sure. Looked like him though. Thought I saw him cross the street." Conan pointed excitedly. "He joined the bus queue."

"Don't let him see us!" commanded John. But just at that moment a Manchester City Bus pulled up to the bus queue, blocking their view.

"Wait!" said Conan. But when the bus pulled away, the queue was empty and a few people were walking away from the bus stop.

"Let's go down to the Clap Hammer to see if he picked up our letter," suggested John.

Hurriedly, they walked the two hundred feet to the pub and pushed open the double doors. The barman was on the telephone, so the boys stood in front of the fire to warm themselves. The barman looked surprised to see them and continued to talk animatedly on the phone, pointing at the boys as though he were talking about them. As soon as he put down the phone he strode over to where they were.

"Your man showed up today. Just left. I was on the phone with the police," he said.

"Did you give him the letter?" asked John in what he hoped was his politest voice.

97

"Sure did! He read it, swore something fierce and threw the letter into the fire. Then he stormed off."

"We saw him," squeaked Alex, hiding behind John.

"If I were you," counseled the barman. "I'd be careful. He swore he'd get that book somehow."

"Yeah, we know," said Conan. "But he'll never get it."

"Now scat! You can't be in here without your parents."

Chapter 36

Finally, on the second Friday in February, on a day with particularly bad weather—driving sleet—Mr. Hume thought it might be a good time to start. Excited that something was happening at last, the boys clattered down the stairs behind Mr. Hume.

They retrieved the broom pole from where it had been safely tucked behind the roaring and clanking furnace. Mr. Hume had to shout over the noise.

"Let's use the lathe. Let me show you."

Mr. Hume mounted the pole on the lathe, which he showed them could be made to run very slowly. He clamped the broom pole in properly, with the big lathe holding the pole at one end and with a ring in the middle to hold it up. This left one end free, hanging out over the floor because the lathe wasn't big enough to hold something that long.

"See, we can turn the machine to wind on the string. Conan, you hold the string tight. Alex, you do the birch twigs. John, you add the willow twigs. I'll operate the machine. Make sure you get your ratio of twigs right!"

And so Conan stood about ten feet back from the lathe, holding the string tight. Mr. Hume had fastened the string to the pole with a small wood screw so it wouldn't slip off. The string was about a foot from the end of the pole, so the twigs extended six inches to a foot beyond the end of the pole. Alex would stick four birch twigs tight under the string, then John would place six willow twigs underneath. They repeated this until they had completely encircled the pole, then Mr. Hume wound an extra loop of string to hold them in place, admonishing Conan to hold the string tight. And then he poured a little carpenter's glue around it, "just to be sure."

It only took them an hour to put so many twigs on that the broom looked positively bushy. After every third layer or so, Mr. Hume had them run several layers of string, so by the time they were done, they had used nearly all of the linen twine.

"Let's put just a little more carpenter's glue to ensure the straw doesn't come off in flight," he said with a wink.

"You still don't believe us, do you?" asked Alex.

"I'm helping you build the broom, right?" replied Mr. Hume with a smile.

Alex didn't say anything.

And so they left it to dry in its safe corner behind the furnace. After all these months, they had a broomstick built exactly to the specifications in the handwritten book. Now all they had to do was make it fly.

Chapter 37

To make it fly, they needed three things. A dead snake. Goat entrails. And Castle Alox. None of them seemed easy. Especially Castle Alox.

But first, they had to get the broom home. The boys held a council in John's room on a very windy first day of March after school. Each had a fizzy drink they'd taken from the Cunningham refrigerator.

"Let's leave right after school. That way we have the most light," suggested Alex.

"But then Marco might see us," objected Conan, taking a sip of his drink with a slight slurp.

"We don't even know if Marco's around," said John.

Alex looked at John over the top of his drink can. "Did the police ever get back to you about what the barman saw?"

"No," reported John. "Nothing. Dad called them too, but this Detective Sergeant Selby guy never called back. Dad says they don't take Marco seriously."

"Maybe we can have your dad be a guard or something," suggested Conan. "I'm sure my dad would, but...." Conan's voice trailed off. John and Alex knew he hadn't seen his dad in five months, with no reports as to his whereabouts.

John knew Alex would've volunteered his dad if he had one.

"Okay, I think that's best. But what if Marco breaks into the house while we're gone? Maybe the broom is safer at school," asked John, turning his drink can idly while thinking.

"But several grown-ups can get into the basement," piped up Alex. "What if Marco bribes one of them?"

Conan laughed. "I doubt it. But I agree it's safest right here. I mean, you can't get through your front door even when you want to!"

So, they asked Mr. Cunningham if he could come home from work early one day and escort them home. But, as it turned out, Dad had a big project with a tight deadline at work, so he was being asked to stay overtime for two weeks. "Maybe after that, boys. I'm sure it's perfectly safe where it is." And so the boys would have to wait.

Chapter 38

Now that the days were longer, Conan had more chances to get outside for casual football with the other boys. On warmer days, John and Alex came out to watch, at least for a while. March weather is fickle, though, and it often rained—chilly, windy, and unpleasant. Every day the boys asked Mr. Hume if the broom was still there. And every day, Mr. Hume told them not to worry.

"Just out of curiosity, what are you going to do with it?" asked Mr. Hume. "It's a long time until Halloween," he said with twinkling eyes, rubbing his palms together. "You put a lot of work into that broom. It's a shame to have it sit down in the basement. Why not bring it up to crafts class and do a show and tell?"

"No!" exclaimed Alex. "It's a secret. Plus, people will think we're doing witchcraft. It's not witchcraft. It's magic!"

"Right, Alex. But didn't the old woman's book say you had to do some things to make it fly? Wasn't there a castle involved?"

"Castle Alox," said Alex.

"Did the book give a map?" asked Mr. Hume, still habitually rubbing his palms together.

"No," said John, answering for Alex. "It just said Castle Alox. You remember the picture, right?"

"Well, if your next step is finding a castle, you'd better get started. Can we look at the picture again? We can do an Internet search on castles because some castle websites have pictures."

"That means we have to bring the old woman's book back to school," said Alex with a shudder.

"Is that a problem?" asked Mr. Hume mildly, looking curiously at Alex. "The thought seems to frighten you."

"It's because of Marco," squeaked Alex.

"Marco?" asked Mr. Hume.

So John, aided occasionally by the other boys, told Mr. Hume all about Marco, including how he had come to Wythenshawe to stalk the boys. "We saw him a few weeks ago just as he left the Clap Hammer."

"And you say you've told the police about this?" asked Mr. Hume incredulously. "And they did nothing?"

"Detective Sergeant Selby finally returned my Dad's call," said John. "But he said they had nothing to go on and couldn't find him."

"We know he's after the book," said Conan, "and probably wants the broom as well. We saw him at Ogden Specialty Woods, too." Conan told them about their Marco sighting. "And so we think he's trying to build a broom, but he doesn't have the book. We don't know where he's getting his information. Maybe he's seen the book in the past. Or maybe," he said darkly, "he forced his sister to tell him!"

"Boys! I had no idea you were being stalked. This puts a whole new dimension on this broomstick project. Are you sure you want to go forward with this?"

"Positively!" piped up Alex. "The old lady told our fortune and said we'd be flying together on a broomstick. We've got the broomstick now. We just need to make it fly!"

Mr. Hume signed and ran his hands through his hair. "Look. I've been humoring you because you wanted to do this so much. But really now, this...."

"It's magic!" insisted Alex. "It'll work! Remember how hard it was to get the book to open!"

"Are you sure it wasn't because you finally jiggled the lock the right way?" said Mr. Hume, disbelievingly.

"We're going forward," said Conan. "We just need to keep the broom and the book away from this Marco guy. Anyway," he went on, "Marco believes it. That's why he wants the book back so badly. He doesn't want to give us any magic secrets."

"But," objected Mr. Hume, "what if Marco does something desperate? What if he kidnaps one of you boys?"

"That's why we've got to hurry!" said Alex. "We've got to do it before he does. He might have a different book or something. You've got to help us!"

"I think I should chat with your parents," said Mr. Hume. "This is more serious than I thought. In the meantime, bring the book in tomorrow and we'll have another look at the castle picture." He seemed deep in thought.

Chapter 39

Sure enough, Mr. Hume called that evening to talk with John's parents. Conan and Alex had already gone to their respective homes and Dad wasn't home yet. The dinner dishes had already been cleared, washed and put away and Katie and John were doing their homework at the big round table in the kitchen. Mum talked with Mr. Hume for quite some time, and all John could hear was what Mum said. The gist of it was that the police thought that Marco would drop his effort with time and was probably not a threat to the boys physically. And, she said, the boys seemed intent on making their broomstick. She thanked Mr. Hume for helping them get this far. She also laughed a little bit, though John couldn't tell what the joke was. And when she was done, she didn't say much to John except to wonder why they'd told Mr. Hume about Marco.

The next day, John pulled the handwritten book out from under the mattress and shoved it into his school bag. He wolfed down breakfast and quickly helped clean up so his Mum and Dad could go to work. As he was just finishing putting away the last dish, the doorbell rang to announce Conan's arrival. And Alex was only a minute later.

"Why are you guys so grim?" asked Katie.

"Nothing," replied Alex grimly.

"Got it?" asked Conan.

"Yep," said John. "Let's go."

A light rain was falling, so they pulled their jacket hoods up over their heads and moved swiftly down Brixton Street in the direction of the school. John felt very vulnerable. He was pretty confident that if Marco met them, he couldn't take the book away from them, given there were three of them and only one of Marco, plus Marco looked pretty old. He was grateful that Conan was there, since Conan was by far the most muscular of the three, given his constant football practices over the winter, even in the bad weather. Marco would be no match for Conan, thought John.

They got to the High Street and waited for the crossing light. Several buses thundered by and other students were gathered around them.

"Marco alert," said Conan.

"Oh no!" exclaimed Alex. "Where?" He looked around frantically.

"Over there by the bus stop in front of the Clap and Hammer," replied Conan. "His back is turned to us now. But I'm sure he saw us!"

John stared intently at the bus stop. All he could think of now was getting into the school safely. The crossing light turned green and the boys ran across, darting between cars that had stopped because of the congestion on the High Street. As they ran across the sidewalk and onto the school property, John glanced to his left in the direction of the bus stop. The pedestrians arranged themselves for just a moment so that John was looking straight at Marco, who was staring back but not moving, pretending to lounge near the bus stop. With a shudder, John ran through the gates and into the school.

Without even talking about it, they ran the length of Sudbury Hall until they came to Mr. Hume's room. Mr. Hume was putting multicolored sheets of construction paper on every desk, chatting happily with two second year girls who looked eager to get started.

"Mr. Hume!" began Alex.

"That man Marco," continued Conan.

"He's outside the school!" finished John.

The second years seemed unhappy to have their conversation interrupted, but as it was sixth years, there wasn't much they could say. They just stood next to Mr. Hume, pouting.

"Show me!" commanded Mr. Hume.

The boys ran the length of New Hall, dodging between students and faculty members now lining up for their first classes, with Mr. Hume following behind. Mr. Hume was by far bigger than any of the boys, so he couldn't make his way through the noisy crowds as fast as the boys could.

At last they burst out onto the street. Conan was there first, his ponytail flying. John was second, Mr. Hume third, and Alex fourth.

But Marco was gone.

"Maybe he's gone into the Clap and Hammer," suggested Alex, holding his side and panting from the exertion.

"The pub's not open yet," said Mr. Hume. "I'll have the office call the police. In the meantime, the bell's about to ring, so you boys should be off to your first period class."

Chapter 40

Detective Sergeant Selby came to visit the school around ten o'clock, pulling John, Conan, and Alex from their class and into the office.

"Are you sure it was him? Did all three of you see him?" he asked.

"I didn't," shuddered Alex. "But Conan and John saw him."

And so Conan and John told him what they could. They also told him about the letter they'd written to Marco, which had caused Marco to fly into a rage before destroying the letter in the Clap and Hammer fireplace. Detective Sergeant Selby told the boys in his most professional voice that it was unwise to attempt any sort of reason with someone who might be stalking them. He asked again why they felt it was so important to keep the book.

Alex led the boys' protests that the old woman wanted them to have the book. But Selby never asked to see the book, and in fact seemed a bit bored by the whole thing.

"Just stick together and don't spend much time wandering the streets. This Marco guy will eventually lose interest. You might think very seriously about your insistence on keeping the book. Marco seems intent on having it as a family heirloom. Why do you want it, anyway?"

John sighed and explained again that the old woman wanted them to have it. He didn't go into the magic part, feeling Selby would just ridicule them. At last, Selby snapped his notebook closed and shooed them back to their classes.

After school, John, Conan and Alex found Mr. Hume sweeping the floor of scraps left behind from all the colored sheets of construction paper. He asked them about the policeman, and John expressed his opinion that the police would never catch Marco.

"Let's look at that castle picture again, shall we?" said Mr. Hume.

John dug down into his school bag and pulled out the book. He flipped it open and swished pages back and forth until he found the right one. He plopped the book on the desk so it was right side up for Mr. Hume. Then the boys crowded around.

"Where is Castle Alox described in the text?" asked Mr. Hume.

"Opposite the picture, right here," replied John, pointing.

The four huddled together, looking at the book. Mr. Hume read it out loud.

"Castle Alox, the most magical castle in the northwest of England and the site of many ancient battles, stands by the sea to guard against the invasion of the Irish. Although not big compared to other castles, it was well-fortified. Not much remains today except the north tower and some of the walls. Place the broomstick on ...." Following this were the instructions for activating the broomstick so it would fly.

"That's not much to go on," said Mr. Hume. "And the borders of what constitutes England have changed considerably over the centuries. In fact, during Castle Alox's prime, there were civil wars and lots of other troubles. Look at the drawing—it would seem to be a modern drawing, since it shows only one tower plus part of a wall sloping away from it. It's too bad she doesn't provide any landscape in the background, as this could give us clues. As you get into Wales, there are mountains, whereas it's flatter as you go north. You pick up some hills in the Lake District, though. Very pretty up there. I've seen some magnificent castle ruins up by Workington."

"So which is Castle Alox?" asked Alex, encouragingly.

"I don't know," replied Mr. Hume. "You've got to search from the Welch border all the way to the Scottish border. That's a couple hundred miles of coastline. Maybe you can find something on the Internet. I can give you the links for some interesting castle sites."

"I know some too!" said Alex proudly. "My mum and I went to some castles last summer so I could see some medieval re-creations." His face fell. "But they were all in Scotland."

"I think you boys have to work on the assumption that your old woman named it Castle Alox for some symbolic reason," said Mr. Hume. "In reality, it might have another name. Look up all the castles you can. And maybe…hmmm…."

The boys looked at him expectantly. He was idly flipping pages back and forth, lost in thought.

After several seconds, John prompted him. "Sir…."

Mr. Hume spoke at last. "When I was at the University of Edinburgh, there was a professor there who seemed to specialize in inventorying old castle ruins. Quite a walking encyclopedia. I'll admit I didn't pay much attention because I was majoring in education with a minor in art history and wasn't interested at that point in castles." Alex looked down at the floor, disappointed. "But since then," continued Mr. Hume, "I've become interested in the architecture because of the art history aspect." Alex looked happier.

"Yes?" prompted John as Mr. Hume trailed off again.

"I don't even know if old Dr. Goole is still alive. He was pretty old back in those days. But I can try to track him down and e-mail him a scan of this drawing. What do you boys think?"

"Yes!" they all replied at once.

So they followed Mr. Hume down to the library and crowded around a computer. Mr. Hume checked the University of Edinburgh at www.ed.ac.uk to see if Dr. Goole was still teaching there. He found a listing for him in the Medieval Studies program in the History Department. In fact, since each professor has a page listing their biography and research interests, they found that Dr. Goole was still teaching and was still interested in castles, especially regarding military history.

So, they used the library scanner to make an electronic copy of the drawing. Mr. Hume logged onto his school e-mail account and composed a message telling them about the school project (without mentioning the broomstick or what they wanted to do) and telling Dr. Goole that they'd unearthed this drawing in an old book and wondered if Dr. Goole might know which castle was the source.

"That's about all I can help you with this afternoon," he said. "I'll leave you to your Internet research."

And so the boys spend the next hour working at the computers in the library. Every so often one of them would call to the others to look at something, but they'd decide the towers they saw on the Internet were either too short or too tall, too broad or too narrow, or had the wrong battlements, or the walls were too big. In fact, after an hour the boys were discouraged.

"I don't think there's anything," said Conan.

"We'll find it," said Alex, but John could tell that he, too, was frustrated and a little discouraged.

Chapter 41

The boys gathered their stuff together and packed their schoolbags. They made their way out of New Hall and onto the rainy courtyard.

"What if Marco is still there?" asked Alex, pulling his jacket hood up over his head.

"I don't see him anywhere," said Conan, who returned from reconnoitering the street.

"Let's go then," said John. "We'll get home before Katie and Miriam."

And so they crossed the High Street, looking in every direction for any sign of Marco, but he wasn't anywhere. They turned onto Brixton Street and walked in the direction of their homes.

"John," said Conan. "I thought you said we'd be the first ones to get home."

"I thought so."

"So why's your door hanging open?"

"Don't know," replied John. "Shouldn't be."

As they rounded the garden and ran up the driveway, John knew something was definitely wrong. The door hadn't merely been opened, it had been forced open! The door jamb was splintered and the casing around the door was broken to pieces. John made to enter but Conan grabbed his jacket sleeve and pulled him back.

"They could still be there," whispered Conan. "Let's go to my house and call the police."

They ran next door to Conan's house. Conan seemed oddly flustered, something not usual for him. John hadn't been in Conan's house in over a year because Conan always seemed to want to come to John's house instead. Conan pulled out his door key and quietly opened the lock. Hesitantly, he stepped inside, seemed indecisive for a moment, then let them in.

His house was a mess. It had the same layout inside as John's, but this was hardly recognizable because of the clutter. There was trash on the floor and hardly any furniture. But what furniture there was turned out to be useless, because the couch and chairs were all piled high with junk—in fact, there was no place to sit down. Newspapers spilled onto the floor from the couch. The old television set was piled with beer and stout cans and other detritus.

"Wait here," said Conan, highly discomfited. "I'll get the portable phone."

Conan stepped across the floor, kicking aside some dirty clothes and several old toys, and went into the kitchen. John and Alex heard something tumble to the floor, but a moment later Conan reappeared with the portable phone without explanation. He silently handed it to John, who dialed 999.

"Hello, my house has been broken into," said John.

"Are you at 12 Brixton Street?" came the voice at the other end of the line. John could hear lots of people in the same room as the voice, all sounding urgent.

"My house is at 14 Brixton Street. I'm next door. We're afraid to go into the house. Maybe the burglar is still there."

"How do you know your house has been broken into then?" asked the voice.

"The door's been smashed in."

"We'll have someone there shortly," said the voice.

They waited several minutes in Conan's doorway for the police to arrive. Conan didn't invite them to come into the house any further, and seemed relieved when they heard the sirens and saw two police cars coming down Brixton Street.

The boys ran out to meet the policemen, who at first thought they were onlookers until John insisted that 14 Brixton Street was his house and he was the one who had called 999. The police made the boys wait inside Conan's house, much to Conan's disappointment, until they'd searched the Cunningham home.

"It's a mess," reported one of the policeman, who came over to tell the boys no one was found inside. The boys followed him out onto the pavement. Alex was shivering. A crowd of onlookers had gathered.

The policeman spoke to him again. "Where are your parents?"

"They're at work," replied John. "Mum should be along any minute. Dad's working overtime."

"Can we call your mum's cell phone?"

"She doesn't have one. She's probably on the Metrolink right now."

"Any brothers or sisters?"

"There's Katie and Miriam. Katie's at her friend's house. Miriam is still in daycare," reported John.

"Come with me then, laddie. Tell me what's missing. And don't touch anything."

Chapter 42

John followed the burly policeman up the steps and through the broken door into the living room. The door creaked and made John jump. Conan followed right behind him, and John could tell by Alex's gasps that he was right on Conan's heels.

The door was wide open now, letting the chill March air into the living room. The couch had been moved away from the wall and the couch cushions were on the floor. Books had been ripped off the bookshelf and strewn onto the floor in a great heap, some reaching all the way across the room to the couch. The television was untouched.

"See anything missing, laddie?" said the policeman. "Usually they take the consumer electronics. I'm surprised the telly is still here."

John shook his head. "I don't know," he muttered, screwing up his courage to look in the kitchen. He set his own school bag down near the couch and Alex did the same. Conan, of course, had left his own school bag at his home when they'd stopped at his house to use the telephone. John stepped into the kitchen to have a look.

If anything, the devastation was more complete. Pots and pans had been turfed out of their safe haven and onto the floor. The spice rack had been pulled out of the cabinet and left on the counter. Piles of cookbooks had been moved from their neat shelves and strewn on the round kitchen table. Two of the chairs had been knocked over.

"I still don't see anything missing," reported John.

"How can you tell, laddie?" asked the policeman, who absentmindedly set a chair upright while his partner was taking photographs.

"Mum just bought that set of pots and pans. There were five. I see five here. She's not going to be happy that one of them is dented."

"Let's take a look at the rest of the house."

One by one, John and the policeman looked in the bedrooms. Mum and Dad's room had been thoroughly wrecked with things strewn everywhere. What particularly interested the burly policeman was that Mum's jewelry box was open but still full of jewelry.

"When does your mum come home, laddie?" he asked.

John glanced at his watch. "Should be any time now," he said.

110

Katie and Miriam's room had most of the contents of the dressers turfed out, but seemed relatively intact. But John's room was a scene of total confusion. The dresser drawers had been pulled out and dumped onto the floor. The dresser itself lay sideways in front of the wardrobe, whose door was open. All John's clothes had been pulled off their hangers and the wardrobe had been moved away from the wall.

And John's bed had been completely unmade. The blankets were on the floor with the bedsheets on top of them. The mattress lay sideways on the box springs, which itself had been detached from the frame.

"This your room, laddie?"

"Yes," said John.

"Looks to me as though the thief was looking for something, laddie. Did they take anything in here?"

"Can I touch things now?" he asked the policeman, who was busy writing in his little black notebook.

"Go ahead. We've already taken photographs. My partner's in the kitchen getting some fingerprints off the shiny bowls in the kitchen. Easy to get prints there," he said.

John pawed through the stuff on the floor. Everything he owned was in that pile, after all. He had a souvenir from last summer's trip to Scotland, plus he had a few books that he'd kept from when he was learning to read, a book about dinosaurs, several toys, and a few video games he didn't want Miriam messing with.

"I don't think anything's missing, sir," reported John. "At least I can't think of anything right now."

They both looked up sharply when they heard a scream outside.

Chapter 43

The policeman bolted into the hallway where all the family pictures were miraculously untouched. John ran behind him, to find Mum clutching Miriam in her arms and crying out frantically.

"John! Katie! What's become of my children!" she screamed. She let Miriam down, who ran to the couch and curled up into a ball.

"Calm down, ma'am!" said the other policeman, pausing from photographing the mess. "Your three boys are here." He motioned to Conan and Alex, who were hovering about, not quite sure what to do.

Mum grabbed John into a rib-splitting hug. It took a few minutes of explaining to tell Mum what John had found, how they'd called for the police, and what they'd found. Mum also had to explain that Conan and Alex weren't her children, which brought a reproachful glance from the policemen, who muttered about how they therefore ought not to be at the scene of the crime. But Mum said it was all right.

The first thing Mum did was call Dad, who said he would hurry home. Mum and the policeman again searched the house to see what might have been missing. Mum reported that £50 she'd left laying on her dresser had been taken, plus a recent photograph of the family, but otherwise everything seemed to be there.

"Do you have any idea who might've done this?" asked the policeman who had the camera.

"Marco!" said John, Conan and Alex at the same time.

"Honey," objected Mum. "He hasn't been around for weeks." She was again carrying Miriam, who was sucking her thumb, something she hadn't done in years. Mum kept pulling Miriam's thumb out of her mouth, but Miriam kept putting it back in.

"We saw him this morning!" said Conan. "At the bus stop in front of the Clap Hammer! The police came to check it out."

"Oh, my!" said Mum, sinking onto a chair next to the couch.

"Who's this Marco fellow?" asked the burly policeman.

John rummaged in his school bag. "Here," he said, giving a business card to the policeman with the camera. "Detective Sergeant Selby knows. Marco's an old man who wants to get a book away from us."

"Is the book safe?" asked the policeman with the camera.

John rummaged more in his schoolbag and produced the handwritten book. "I took it to school today for a school project."

The burly policeman looked it over. "All about magic, eh?" He handed it back to John. "I'd think you could get that on the Internet. Why's he so interested?"

John, helped by Conan and particularly Alex, related the story of finding the handwritten book. But he neatly left out the part about actually building the broomstick, or the fact that it lay finished in the forbidden basement in Old Hall.

"You boys shouldn't have left that letter at the Clap Hammer. It just encouraged him," said the policeman with the camera. "We'll be in touch with Detective Sergeant Selby to compare notes. I'm afraid this Marco fellow might be hard to track down. We'll wait until your father comes, then we'll be off. Ma'am," he said, looking at Mum. "Could we just get your fingerprints so we can compare yours with the thief's?"

Dad came along not long after, and the boys told their story yet again. Dad was miffed that the boys hadn't called him at work after the Marco sighting, but was relieved to hear they'd at least told Mr. Hume. They spent the rest of the evening cleaning up the house as well as they could, with Conan and Alex staying to help until Mum finally shooed them away, telling them they needed to get their homework done.

John didn't think this was a good time to approach Dad about helping them find Castle Alox.

John hadn't dared even bring up the subject of the handwritten book, which was now stored in Alex's bedroom at the bottom of an old wardrobe—John thought it best to get it out of the Cunningham house for several reasons—not the least of which was that it might attract Marco again. But Marco did not show up anywhere, nor did the police have any leads. The fingerprints were in fact traced to Marco Stoney, who had been arrested for burglary some two decades before and released for lack of any evidence linking him directly to the crime.

"Whereabouts unknown," said Dad over dinner at the round table in the Cunningham kitchen. "You'd think in this day and age they could find a man," he grumbled.

"I don't like thinking he's on the loose. What did he want with a family picture?" said Mum, sipping on her hot soup. "I'm just glad he didn't take my mum's ring."

Chapter 44

Dr. Goole's reply came two weeks after the break-in at the Cunningham house. Mr. Hume told the boys to come back after school. All three showed up, which proved Conan's interest, since there was regular football team practice after school now that the weather was starting to warm up.

"I just want to see it, then I've got to go to practice," he said in response to Alex's query.

Mr. Hume led them to the library, where he logged into his e-mail account. The boys hovered around to read.

"I'm glad to see you're taking an interested in our military history after twenty years," said Dr. Goole. "I recall you once told me that all the castle walls in the country could come tumbling down, as long as they preserved the art."

"At least he remembers me," said Mr. Hume.

"Your drawing does not match any castle that I can think of right off hand. But the battlements appear to date from the twelfth century. There are five castles along the northwestern English coast from the same time period. I don't have enough photographs to say definitively whether they are or are not the castle shown in the drawing. There is one four miles east of Wallasey on A540, partially restored, one at Southport, mostly ruins, the old one at Fleetwood, again, mostly ruins, the excellent one at Morecambe, now a private dwelling—hard to get a viewing—and finally one St. Bees Head south of Workington that's open in the summertime."

Alex looked the most excited. "So all we have to do is check these out. Do you have any pictures of any of these?" he asked.

"I think you boys need to do some research," warned Mr. Hume. "And, you'd better check these out before you go. I have a few pictures of Wallasey, but none of the others. Here's what I have," he said, spreading four photographs on the table.

The pictures showed a castle on a gray day—the entrance, now restored, the tourist shop, inside the partially restored great hall, and a couple views from the top of one of the towers. Unfortunately, there were no pictures of any of the towers.

"Sorry, boys, I was more interested in the restoration work, so I didn't look much at the towers. But I'm not sure this is your castle anyway."

"So all we have to do," said John, "is get Dad to drive us to these castles. We can walk around them and check them out. Do you think we can do this in one day?"

"It's a bit of a drive," said Mr. Hume. "But a couple Saturdays, maybe?"

Their research on the Internet turned up a few photographs, but it seemed these castles were not as important as those further inland, so most didn't have preservation societies behind them, except for the one Mr. Hume mentioned at Wallasey, and it looked from the pictures on the Wallasey website as though this were a pretty small castle. Fortunately, they found driving instructions for all the castles, which they carefully printed out, as Dad would need these.

Chapter 45

And so, on the last Saturday in March, Dad and the boys were in the old Jaguar heading along M62 from Manchester to Liverpool in a light rain on a gray day. At least they were past the vernal equinox, so now the days were slightly longer than the nights. Dad had his new digital camera along just in case they found anything interesting. He hadn't been terribly interested in driving them around to see castles, given as Mum still had the jitters from the break-in, but Mum agreed to stay home with Katie and Miriam while Dad took the boys. And since they were leaving early in the morning, Conan and Alex slept over. This time, John remembered why he was waking up, and didn't step on either Conan or Alex as he got out of bed.

They took with them a printout of the scanned drawing from the handwritten book, since they wanted the old book to be safe at Alex's house. John had it folded up in his pocket, but now he pulled it out and studied it carefully.

"It looks like the only thing standing is the tower," he said, handing the drawing to the back seat where Alex took it. "And that little bit of wall." He twisted around in his seat to face Alex and Conan. "You can just see a little bit of the old wall on the other side. Looks like it's barely above ground level."

"You don't know when that drawing was made," warned Dad. "There might have been considerable restoration work done since."

"It doesn't look very big," said Alex. "The tower is only three stories tall. At least that's the way it looks from the slits where the archers used to hide. See, here?" And he pointed to the tower itself.

Dad stopped to pay the toll for the bridge over the Mercy River that connects Liverpool with Birkenhead. After fighting some traffic, they were in Wallasey and turned left.

"Four miles, you say?" he asked.

John pulled out the driving directions. "We go past M53 and turn right on A540. Then two miles and it will be on the right."

They pulled into a small car park in the wooded setting around the castle and got out of the car. The boys pulled their hoods over their heads and Dad opted for an umbrella.

"Not very big, is it?" said Conan.

"I don't think this is the right one," piped up Alex.

"Let's walk all the way around it," said John. "Maybe it looks different from the back."

They paid their admission at the gate so they could get onto the castle grounds. A gruff fellow took their £1 apiece and gave them a map of the grounds. Indeed, the building had been partially restored, with most of the work done on the great hall. There was a path around the interior of the walls, which they took, with Alex leading the way. The walls themselves were mostly gone and what was left was covered in moss. They could see where three circular towers had stood, and a fourth ruined tower still stood, but only about ten feet high. A side path led inside it, so the boys clambered in. There was nothing inside.

"This isn't it," sighed John. "Not even close."

"Can we peek inside the great hall?" asked Alex. "It looked cool on the Internet."

"We've come this far," answered Dad. "Just a few minutes."

116

So Alex, practically dancing, led the way into the great hall, which wasn't so great after all. The restorers had put a roof over the top with massive wooden beams and the windows had been placed, but there was no heat, so it was chilly inside. The complete structure wasn't much bigger than perhaps twice the size of John's house. There were some exhibits that showed what castle life was like back in medieval times, with a few dioramas to give a better idea. John decided he liked his house better. There was a collecting tin near the door for those who wanted to make more donations. All told, Alex gave them more information about medieval life than the placards did.

"Boys, I think we've seen all we can see here. Let's be off to Southport."

And so they clambered into the car and drove off. They re-crossed the Mercy and drove into Liverpool and took the large roundabout to the left and headed up through Bootle. They were finally out of the big city about the time they reached Formby on A565. They never really got into scenery that was fully countryside, since there were houses and businesses along the highway. They followed John's printed driving instructions until they came to the castle at Southport.

It turned out the Southport castle had been built on a rise overlooking the sea. There was a tiny car park near the ruins from which they could see everything. The weather was clearing up; it had stopped raining and the sun occasionally peeked out through the clouds. But, apart from bits of the wall that went up about waist high, the castle was completely in ruins. Nothing even looked like a tower except some circular foundation stones about knee height. They didn't even get out of the car.

"That was a disappointment," said Dad, voicing what they all felt.

"Are you sure we're in the right place?" asked Conan.

"We followed the driving instructions exactly. Wait a minute, Dad! There's a sign over there. Hang on!"

John dashed out of the car, slopping through a small puddle to read the sign and then dashed back to the car.

"Southport Castle," he reported breathlessly. "Built 1159, destroyed in a siege in 1392."

"I'm surprised even this much is left," said Dad as they pulled away. "Where's the next one?"

"Fleetwood. And Dr. Goole said it was mostly ruins, too."

"But there could still be a tower standing," suggested Alex optimistically.

To get to Fleetwood they continued up the highway until they came into Preston, where the traffic was heavy. They hopped onto M55 and drove to Exit 3, which they took north, taking back roads into Fleetwood. The area is fairly heavily populated, so it was after noon when they arrived. Dad suggested lunch, but the boys were too interested in seeing the castle, so they drove on following John's driving instructions. They made one false start and had to backtrack to get where they needed to be.

The castle, as it turned out, was in a large town park in Fleetwood itself. As they parked, they could see a tower through the trees, and excitement was high as Dad locked the door. There was no admission charge this time. The park was full of people walking, children laughing, with everyone out now that the sun had come out fully. The boys kept their jackets on, but unzipped them. Alex fairly skipped down the path.

As it turned out, Dr. Goole was exactly right; the castle was mostly ruins. No preservation society was trying to restore anything, either. One tower was still standing, though it was ruined with no top. The boys clambered inside and once again found it empty; they had a view of the sky once inside.

Disappointed, they didn't say anything as Dad drove around looking for a hamburger restaurant. They opted for a large pub with a car park.

"How many more?" asked Dad as he bit into his big, juicy hamburger.

"Just two," replied John, spreading out the driving directions.

"Can I look at the map?" asked Dad. John pushed it in his direction. "I think we have time for Morecambe, but then we really need to get back. We'll have to do St. Bees Head another Saturday and get an early start."

The boys were disappointed, but said nothing.

After lunch, Dad drove the big Jaguar north again along A588 toward Lancaster; they followed John's driving directions. They got lost in Lancaster and had to stop at a petrol station to ask for directions, which took the man a few minutes to figure out based on John's printout. After consulting a large map he had, the man amended John's driving directions with some extra details and they were soon on their way.

Indeed, the castle was a private residence, just as Dr. Goole had said. It was set on a large estate overlooking the Irish Sea with large formal gardens complete with topiaries. The public road ran around it, so they drove around the castle three times while the boys compared it to the drawings.

"I can't tell where it's been modified," said Conan, puzzled.

"It's big!" said John. "I wish we could all live in a place like that!"

"I wouldn't want to pay the heating bills," said Dad. "Nor have to clean it."

"It's not the right place," said Alex with finality.

"How do you know?" asked Conan.

"It's too tall," said Alex. "The towers are five stories each. And the battlements aren't right."

They pulled to the side of the road near the gates where they had a view of the towers. Dad studied the drawing carefully.

"I think you're right, Alex. And this castle looks as though it's pretty much intact. The one in the drawing is a ruin except for the tower," said Dad.

"Can we go up to St. Bees Head?" asked John.

"We're already late getting back," said Dad. "We'll have to reserve St. Bees Head for another day."

"Bummer," said Alex.

Chapter 46

On Monday the boys reported their findings to Mr. Hume after school in the crafts room.

"We have one to go," said Alex. "St. Bees Head. It has to be the one!"

"Only one left," said Conan.

But Mr. Hume had a twinkle in his eye. "I may have something for you. Follow me down to the library."

And he wouldn't say another word until they followed him to the library. He led the way to one of the computers, logged into his school e-mail account, and had them read the screen.

"Jack," the e-mail said. "There is another possibility. I know you said it would be in northwest England, but there is a castle in Wales that may fill the bill. It's about fifteen miles east of Rhyl, closer to Hollywell really. Not much there. All that remains is a tower and part of one wall. The rest is ruins. One of my graduate students stumbled on it after I mentioned your e-mail to him. I've attached a photograph he took last summer on a field trip studying Welch castles. It's not quite from the same angle as the drawing, but you'll see that the battlements are identical and it looks as though the wall remnant could fit into the same jigsaw puzzle."

Mr. Hume opened the attached image and the boys gasped. It was clearly the same wall. John fished the drawing printout from his school bag and held it up near the screen.

"That's the one!" exclaimed Alex.

"Identical," said Conan, pointing at the windows.

"It's got to be," agreed John.

Mr. Hume grinned. "Stroke of good luck, I'd say."

That evening, Dad agreed they could check it out the following Saturday. "So close to Wallasey," he said. "We were going in the wrong direction entirely."

Chapter 47

But something happened on Thursday to take their minds off the castle.

"Marco alert," whispered Conan.

The boys had just crossed the High Street on their way home from school.

"Where?" exclaimed John and Alex together.

"Down the High Street. Back that way." He pointed in the direction opposite from the Clap Hammer Pub.

The road was crowded because it was nearing rush hour. The boys had stayed behind so Conan could play in a pre-season game between Allerton Primary and Alwoodley Primary, the nearest primary school. Conan had scored two of the goals and

120

helped beat Alwoodley soundly, which John and Alex found very exciting, even if it were a preseason game that didn't count toward the championship. Alex was still a little hoarse from yelling so much.

"I have the castle drawing with me!" said John. "If he catches us and takes my school bag, he'll know which castle."

"What do we do?" said Alex. "He'll follow us home again."

"I'm amazed he's showing his face!" exclaimed Conan. "We all know he broke into your house."

"Let's go down to the pub and call the police," said John. "Follow me."

And so they ran down the street, dodging in and out of pedestrians. "Come on, Alex!" shouted Conan.

"You run too fast!" squeaked Alex.

John and Conan reached the pub's double doors long before Alex. They waited there for him, then they burst into the pub.

"You again!" said the barman gruffly. "You're more trouble than you're worth! What's up now?"

"That man!" puffed Alex. "Marco! He's stalking us again!"

"Oh is he now?" said the barman, coming out from behind the bar. "Where is he?" The barman strode out through the double doors onto the street and came back a moment later. "I don't see him."

Conan pointed at the window. "There he is!"

John, Alex and the barman swiveled around. Sure enough, Marco was standing at the window looking in. And he didn't stop looking in when he saw the boys looking back at him either. The barman strode out the double doors. Tentatively, the boys followed, still holding onto their school bags.

"Get on your way, you lousy pest!" shouted the barman. "Leave these boys alone!"

"I want that book! It's mine!"

"You broke into our house!" shouted John. "You're a thief!"

"He what?" said the barman. "He broke into your house!"

"I want that book!" shouted Marco, sounding deranged. "It's no crime to take what's mine!"

"Boys, inside! I'm calling the police!"

But Marco lunged at John and grabbed his school bag. "You have the book! I know you have the book! It's mine!"

John fought with all his strength, both arms around his school bag. The handwritten book was not inside, of course, but the drawing of Castle Alox was. Marco got hold of a strap and tugged, yanking it back and forth. A crowd was gathering.

"Give me my school bag!" shouted John.

"See here, fellow!" said a burly bystander. "Give the boy his school bag!"

"He's a thief!" roared Marco. "He has my book!"

"It's not true!" yelled John. "Give me my bag!"

The barman jumped between John and Marco and grabbed the school bag. Marco looked as though he was mental and crazed enough to have another go, but the barman seized him by his shirt and pulled him away.

"Leave the boys alone, Marco!" he yelled. "You're going to the cops!"

Marco struggled wildly until the barman lost his grip. The old man darted between the onlookers and ran down the street, jumping onto a bus that was just pulling away.

"How did he find us?" asked Alex.

"Weird," said Conan, helping John straighten his sweater.

"Maybe you boys should come inside. We need to tell that Selby fellow that Marco is back in the area," said the barman, who held the door open for them.

Chapter 48

This time the barman didn't give them any trouble about staying. They sat in a booth where they could see the double doors. The barman called Detective Sergeant Selby. Then John used the phone to call his mum at work to tell her where they were.

Selby came by twenty minutes later and listened to their story. The barman came over to add his part, bringing fizzy drinks for the boys. Selby hadn't heard that the Cunningham house had been broken into. He promised to check it out.

"Shame he got away," he said. "Why's he so interested in this book?"

"We told you last time," said Conan.

But John reiterated the story of the handwritten book. "Oh, yes," said Selby, mildly interested.

"I had it with me the day Marco broke into our house."

"You're sure it was this Marco guy?" asked Selby.

"They matched his fingerprints!" exclaimed Alex.

"Why don't you boys wait here until your parents can pick you up?" suggested Selby. "We'll keep a lookout for Marco Stoney."

"How are you going to find him," challenged Conan.

"We'll keep a lookout," repeated Selby.

"How come you haven't found him already?" pressed Conan.

"Slippery character. I'd be careful if I were you boys," said Selby enigmatically.

So the boys waited until both Mum and Dad came to the pub with Katie and Miriam to get them. Dad bought them all dinner at the pub and expressed his thanks to the barman. And John gave the drawing printout to Conan to take home so there would be nothing to interest Marco at the Cunningham's house.

Chapter 49

Dad, John, Conan and Alex left the Cunningham's at ten o'clock on the first Saturday in April and drove along M56 to the west. After discussing over and over again how Marco could be finding them all the time, they decided it was just a fluke and he must have been watching for them to leave the school.

"Why don't the police just post someone outside the school?" asked Conan.

"Maybe they have, just on different days," suggested Dad.

"He scares me," said Alex.

After exhausting this topic, they turned to discussing Allerton's chances in the upcoming football tournament. This conversation occupied Dad, John, and Conan—Conan particularly—but Alex was quiet and thoughtful, fingering the Castle Alox drawing.

The motorway ended. They turned left onto A550 and made another turn to the right as soon as they crossed into Wales, following along the river and then along the seashore. They drove through Holywell.

"Four miles more," said John, looking up from the driving directions he'd copied down from the Internet. "The real name of the castle is Roxhall, if this is the right place."

The four miles took them fifteen minutes, given they were passing directly in front of homes and the occasional pub along the seashore. The country was mildly hilly, although they could see taller mountains in the sunny distance.

The castle, as it turned out, was on a small bluff overlooking the Irish Sea to the north. They pulled into the car park some ways from the castle. There was no one else there. Alex was out of the car in a flash, running down the path toward the ruins. Conan ran after him, his ponytail flying, determined not to let Alex beat him in any running contest. John and Dad hurried down the path.

As soon as they rounded the corner, they knew they had found the castle. All that stood was one tower and part of one wall. The rest was ruins, the rock long carted away by villagers in centuries past who had used the old castle as a convenient source of building materials. Alex ran down the hill to a rocky bluff overlooking the sea, holding the drawing in his hands. He stood on the rock and looked back.

"The drawing was done from right here!" he yelled over the sound of the surf. "This is it!"

Conan was at his side in an instant and grabbed the printout. "This is it!" he yelled.

John pulled the printout from Conan's hands and compared it with the scene in front of them. Indeed, the tower and wall section matched the drawing in every way. The same battlements, the archer's windows in the same spots, the damaged wall matching stone for stone.

"Well boys," exclaimed Dad, "I truly didn't think this possible. You've found your castle!"

The boys ran back to the ruin and popped inside the tower and looked up. Someone had built a roof, and there were rickety wooden stairs that led to the top.

"I'm the lightest," volunteered Alex. "Let me go up first."

He was almost to the top when Dad joined them. "Alex!" he exclaimed. "Is it safe to go up there?"

But Alex didn't seem to hear him. He disappeared through the hole in the roof and they heard him tromping about on top above the noise from the sea. In a moment his head reappeared. "It's fine up here. This looks new!"

And before Dad could stop them, John and Conan raced up the rickety stairs, careful to keep close to the wall, as the handrail didn't look solid in places. They jumped through the hole and out onto the top.

"Wow, you can see for a long ways," said Conan.

"So all we have to do is come here the night of the full moon," said John.

"It's pretty deserted. Marco will never find us here!" said Alex confidently.

"This place feels a little weird, doesn't it?" said Conan.

"Yeah, weird like when the old lady had us touch her palm," replied John.

Chapter 50

"We found the castle," said John, Conan, and Alex together when they saw Mr. Hume in the crowded hallway on Monday. But Mr. Hume barely had time to say "Cool!" when the bustling students swept them by.

"When's the full moon?" they asked when they saw him again after school, once again putting away paint brushes.

Mr. Hume looked at the calendar. "Last Saturday in April," he said.

The boys groaned. "That's a couple weeks away!" said Conan.

"So you have your castle," said Mr. Hume. "How are you doing on goat entrails and a snake?" he asked with the usual twinkle seeming even larger. "Are you really going through with this?"

"Of course!" said the boys. Alex continued. "The book was right, wasn't it? There really was a castle that looked just like the book."

Mr. Hume smiled. "Anyone can draw a picture of a castle and name it anything they want. Now you're talking real magic here. And doesn't it have to be during a thunderstorm?"

"There has to be lightning. But we get lots of thunderstorms this time of year!" said Alex.

"It's not safe to be standing atop a castle tower during a thunderstorm," warned Mr. Hume.

"We don't have to stand on it. Just put the broomstick up there and then wait to see if there's a lightning strike."

"You're determined to see this through, aren't you?" said Mr. Hume as he was sorting brushes on his desk.

"You can't stop helping us now!" exclaimed Conan.

Mr. Hume looked at the boys seriously. "I don't want you wandering about unprotected during a thunderstorm. Do you hear me?"

The boys looked at each other. John replied for them. "Of course not! And we'll have Dad with us."

"Ok, then," said Mr. Hume. He sighed. "You can probably get goat entrails from a specialty meat butcher, or maybe from a goat farmer. The snake is more problematic. I know a high school science teacher over at Whetherby. Sometimes they dissect snakes in their biology classes. We might get one that way. I think you need to look up specialty meats in the telephone book."

But the goat entrails problem turned out to be a hard one to solve. They called no fewer than five specialty butcher shops. "I've got goat for sure!" said one man. "But the entrails? I can get you goat intestines if you're thinking about stuffing your own sausage. Is that what you're doing?"

"Not sure. It's for a school project. I think we need all the goat entrails," said John.

"Can't help you then," said the man, who promptly hung up.

After a couple afternoons of this, John discussed the problem with Mum. She suggested calling Aunt Emma, because she knew relatives who lived on a farm. Maybe they could help? So John called her. She didn't give John much of a chance to talk about goat entrails right away, but wanted to know how he was doing at school. And, she wanted to know about Conan and Alex. Finally, John was able to pose his question about needing goat entrails "for a school project." Aunt Emma wanted to know all about what sort of project this might be. John frantically thought of what he could say, but Aunt Emma saved him the trouble by

126

saying it must be for his science class. She said she had a grandson who worked on a farm, and promised to call him to see what he could come up with.

By the middle of April, John, Conan, and Alex were getting worried. The full moon would be the third Saturday of the month, according to Mr. Hume's calendar, so they were running out of time. Mr. Hume assured them he would probably have a garden snake on time from his buddy at Whetherby High School, which the boys would be attending the following year, but still they hadn't heard from Aunt Emma. So, on the Wednesday evening prior to the full moon, John badgered Mum into calling Aunt Emma. This time Mum spoke to her. Mum told her that the boys had opened the handwritten book, but didn't spell out the connection between the book, the broomstick, and the goat entrails, for which John was grateful. Somehow he thought his chances of getting goat entrails would be less if Aunt Emma knew it was for something magic.

Finally, after what seemed like endless side conversations, Mum got the news that John's second cousin, Irwin Grant, whom John had never met, worked at a dairy outside of Northwich, not that far from Manchester. Aunt Emma had talked to him and told him that John would be calling about his school project. In fact, Aunt Emma insisted, she'd left a message on the Cunningham telephone about this, but Mum said "perhaps one of the children erased it accidentally."

And so John called his second cousin Irwin, who turned out to be a lot older than he was, nearly 30. Irwin wanted to know all about John, so it took a long time to get around to goat entrails. John crossed his fingers when they finally got to the subject. Yes, said Irwin, they slaughtered about one goat a week; in fact, they were sending one to the butcher the following day. Could they keep at least some of the entrails for John? It was for a school project. Irwin said he'd speak to his supervisor.

Dad, by now resigned to taking the boys back to Holywell on Saturday, spoke to Irwin. They'd pick up the entrails and put them in an ice chest on the way to Holywell.

Katie kept screwing up her nose and saying "eew" every time the word 'entrails' was mentioned.

And Mr. Hume told them to stay after school on Friday. Conan had a football game, but John and Alex hurried to Mr. Hume's classroom in New Hall. They followed him across the courtyard and into the science classroom in Old Hall, where Mr. Hume spoke to the teacher there, Mr. Lutterworth, who smiled at the boys and pulled a paper bag out of the science lab refrigerator. He handed it to Mr. Hume who handed it to the boys.

John peeked inside the bag. Inside the paper bag was a sealed plastic bag. And inside the plastic bag was a coiled up, very dead, plain old-fashioned garden snake.

"I'll bet your mum won't enjoy having that in the refrigerator," said Mr. Hume with a twinkle in his eye as they walked across the courtyard.

Chapter 51

Since they didn't need to be at Castle Alox until nine o'clock on Saturday evening, the boys didn't leave Brixton Street until noon. This gave John, Conan and Alex plenty of time to be nervous. Conan mostly wanted to relive the game of the previous day (Allerton had beaten Pershore Primary School handily and Conan had scored three of the goals) and Alex had his nose buried in the handwritten book, which he'd brought over that morning. John kept looking at the clock to see what time it was.

Mum fed them hot, steaming soup and some cheese sandwiches. "Bit of a chill today," she said. "Best take your coats along."

The first thing John noticed as they headed south out of Manchester in the old Jaguar was that the weather was excellent. Chilly, yes. Windy, yes. But the sky was clear and the sun shone through the car windows as they drove toward Northwich.

"What's the weather forecast, Dad?" asked John.

"Clear and cold."

"But we need lightning!"

Dad smiled. "We'll just have to see, won't we."

They stopped at the dairy in Northwich, which turned out to be near the intersection of A49 and A556. John had never been to a dairy before. Irwin gave the boys a tour and John could tell that Irwin was very proud of the work they did there. One of the goats seemed to take a particular interest in Conan, continually butting him, so Conan butted him back.

"Best goat cheese in a hundred miles!" boasted Irwin. "Want to sample some?"

The boys took some and tried to put on their most polite faces, even though they all thought it was horrible. Besides, they always ate cheese with something else, like crackers, and Irwin just offered it to them plain.

"What are you boys doing with the goat entrails?" asked Irwin.

"School project," replied John vaguely. That seemed to satisfy Irwin.

"Keep these on ice," said Irwin, handing two yucky-looking bags to John and Alex to carry. "Did you bring an ice chest?"

"Yes," replied Dad. "If you have some more crushed ice, that would be most helpful."

"We've got plenty," said Irwin. "Ice machine over here. Help yourself."

So Dad took the ice chest out of the back of the old Jaguar and plopped it on the ground near the ice machine. He put some ice in the bottom, put in the two bags of squishy entrails, then covered them with ice.

They left the dairy about four o'clock and headed to Holywell. Soon they were at the Holywell Inn, a pub that also offered rooms. Dad took care of the transaction and got the key to their room, Number 3, which overlooked the Irish Sea.

"Nice room," said the gal behind the bar. She looked to be middle aged and rather big around the middle. "You have a nice view. We don't get many people this time of year—still too cold. What brings you to Holywell?"

"The boys have a school project," said Dad, eyeing John.

"What's that, young man?" asked the lady. "You boys don't look like brothers."

John thought she was too inquisitive. "We're going to look at the old castle out of town. The one right by the sea that's west of here."

"Oh, that place?" said the rotund lady. She leaned down and spoke in a stage whisper. "That place gives me the creeps, it does. A mad duke, that's what they say what lived there. Not much left now."

"What's the name of the place?" asked Conan.

"Oh, we just call it Roxhall Castle. But there was some gentleman in here a couple days ago asking about it. He stayed in Room 2, he did. Not a great tipper, nor did he drink much." She grimaced. "He called it Castle Alox, he did. Weird name."

The boys looked at each other.

"Do you remember his name?" ventured Dad very casually.

"What are you on about? Are you the police?" asked the lady, waving her hand and nearly hitting Alex on the head. "I don't give away the names of my customers, I don't!"

"Was it Marco Stoney?" asked John quietly.

"Nope. Said his name was John Smith." She leaned over, using her stage whisper again while patting John on the shoulder. "I don't think that was his real name, though. But he was real interested in the castle place. Asked all sorts of questions about it. Said he had to visit it in the moonlight. Strange bloke. Drove away at ten at night and didn't come back until one in the morning."

"Uh…" was all John could stammer. "Did he get what he was looking for? I'm just curious," he hastened to add, since the woman was looking mutinous.

"Nope! He was all angry yesterday morning at breakfast. Kept asking me when the full moon was, like he was a werewolf or something. Kind of reminded me of one. I told him he was one day early, he was." She leaned down conspiratorially. "Full moon's tonight," she said, looking around. "We get some loonies here during the full moon."

"It's interesting to find someone else interested in the castle," said Dad. "I don't suppose this man is still around." The boys looked at him. "I was just thinking we could compare notes."

"He just said it had to be within three days of the full moon. I thought he was raving. He said he had to get back to Leeds—said his wife was expecting him."

Chapter 52

Once dad and the boys got to their room on the second floor and shut the door, the boys burst out talking.

"How'd he find out about Castle Alox?" asked Alex.

"How'd he know about the full moon?" asked Conan.

"Maybe there's another book," suggested Dad.

"I'll bet he forced his sister to tell him!" stated John. "Probably beat it out of her!"

"John! We know nothing of the sort," said Dad soothingly. "And the handwritten book looks like the fifty-year-old book that Aunt Emma has, so the broomstick chapter could have been written long ago."

It took the boys a long time to settle down. They whiled away their time after dinner by watching television and reviewing their action plan. At ten o'clock, they walked down the stairs, out the pub door, and to the waiting old Jaguar. The four mile drive along the coast only took a few minutes.

"There's hardly a cloud in the sky," commented Dad as they drove into the completely empty car park. "It's a good thing there's a full moon, because there's no other light."

Looking around for any sign of Marco, the boys clambered out of the car. John carefully removed the finished broomstick and held it with the twigs up high so they wouldn't scrape against the ground and get broken. There was no hint of a breeze. They could hear a few waves lapping at the rocks below them, but otherwise everything was deathly still.

"Alex, here," whispered Dad as he opened the trunk and undid the latch on the ice chest. "Here's your bag of entrails. Maybe just one bag?"

"Why are you whispering?" whispered Conan.

"Don't know," laughed Dad. "Just seems like the thing to do. This is the magic moment, right?" He pulled the plastic bag containing the snake out of the ice chest and gave it to Conan. "All right, boys. I'll wait here for you. Yell if you need me."

John took Dad's torch in his right hand and the broomstick in his left. The torch was unnecessary, given the blinding brightness of the full moon, completely unshielded by any clouds. The boys ran down the path to the castle. Once at the entrance to the tower, John lit the torch and played it around the inside. It looked just as it had on their last visit: empty except for the staircase. Moonlight streamed in the entryway and from the windows up the inside of the tower.

"It's weird in here!" exclaimed Alex. "Like it's sort of whispering to us."

"You're imagining things," said Conan, though he didn't sound convinced.

John crept up the stairs.

"I can't see!" hissed Alex. "Shine the torch back here."

"Don't drop the entrails," cautioned Conan. "Stay close to the wall."

Once John came out atop the tower, he shined the torch down the staircase so Conan and Alex could come out on top. Fortunately, no one had dropped anything on their way to the top.

"Ugh! What's this stuff?" asked Conan. "Shine the light over here," he said, pointing to a spot nearest the sea.

"Yuck! Looks like intestines!" exclaimed Alex.

"So Marco's already been here!" said John. He put the broom down on the wood. "I wonder," he said. "It just said put goat entrails and the snake on the broom and wait for the lightning to hit. We really don't need to take it out of the plastic bags, I think."

Alex plopped his bag of entrails over the ash broom handle, squishing the bag around so it would stay put. Conan did likewise with the snake bag.

"I hope this works," said Conan. "It really does feel odd up here."

John relit the torch and the boys went down the stairs and back to the car, which was easy in the bright moonlight. Dad was leaning against the car when they got back.

"Marco's been here!" exclaimed Conan. "He left entrails behind. Kind of gross, really."

The boys clambered into the car. All they could do now was wait to see if lightning would strike the old tower. After about a half hour, John heard Alex start to snore gently. When his watch said eleven o'clock, Conan's raspy breath told John that Conan had gone to sleep too. And John didn't remember anything after that until he felt his father's gentle hand on his shoulder.

"John," whispered Dad. "It's two in the morning. "Nothing happened."

It took John a moment to orient himself. He stretched, his hands hitting the top of the car. "You're sure?" he muttered.

"I would've heard the thunder. You boys better go retrieve your stuff. We can't leave it here."

So a very sleepy John, Conan, and Alex wandered up the path in the bright moonlight, their shadows stretching before them. They climbed the stairs reluctantly. The broomstick was exactly where they'd left it a few hours before. Alex picked up the plastic bag of entrails, Conan picked up the snake, and John picked up the broomstick. The three glumly trooped down the stairs to the light of Dad's flashlight.

Chapter 53

On Monday afternoon, the boys reported their progress, or really the lack of it, to Mr. Hume. "We did everything we were supposed to, but no lightning strike," said Alex, as though Mr. Hume could order up a lightning strike at will.

Mr. Hume surveyed the boys. "The forecast was for good weather. Still good, in fact," he said, pointing to the windows. "The days are getting longer now, too." He smiled. "Perhaps you'll have better, I mean worse, weather during the May full moon."

"I don't think Dad's real eager to give it another go," reported John, looking at the floor. "I think he did it just to humor us."

"He let us sleep in until ten o'clock!" chimed in Alex.

"And he said 'better luck next time!'" objected Conan.

"Yeah, well, that's not what he said to me last night," said John in a small voice.

"You didn't tell us anything," said Conan, looking askance at John.

"Dad said he doesn't think there's any real magic," said John. "So, anyway, we have four weeks to convince him we want another go."

Chapter 54

The next month had nothing to do with our story, except for a brief Marco sighting, and Conan wasn't absolutely sure. "I'm seeing Marco everywhere," he said, shaking his head. But the boys were very busy, given May was the last month they'd be spending at Allerton Primary School. They had projects to finish, essays to write, tests to take, and all the things that were otherwise required to wrap up the school year. And football season was in full swing. Now that the weather was finally warm and the tulips bloomed everywhere, Conan was constantly on the go with football games and practice. Thanks largely to Conan's efforts, Allerton was first in its league and doing very well indeed. And on one memorable and quite warm and sunny afternoon, the coach from the Wythenshawe High School team took Conan aside and told him that he hoped he'd enter his name for the high school football team. Conan's smile was particularly broad that day as they walked home from school together.

One thing that cheered the boys greatly was Mr. Hume's news that he was transferring from Allerton Primary School in the fall to Wythenshawe High School to teach art.

John, Conan and Alex never thought they'd be hoping for bad weather, but as the fourth Saturday approached, they kept an eye on the forecast. They had mixed feelings, since the graduation ceremony was slated for the morning along with a luncheon for all the parents. On the Sunday before the graduation, John broached the question.

"Dad, if the weather's bad on Saturday, can we have another go?"

Dad chewed his dinner in silence. He seemed far away, lost in thought. He glanced at Mum and put down his fork.

"You're not going again!" objected Katie. "How come you take John places and you don't take the girls?"

"Yeah," piped up Miriam.

"We got this far!" said John, putting down his fork too.

Dad looked at the calendar hanging on the wall. "The full moon is Friday."

"But we can do it up to three days away from the full moon!" interjected John. "And we kept the entrails and the snake in the freezer, so we still have those!"

"They're taking up a lot of freezer space, dear," said Mum. "I'd like to get rid of them."

"I think we'd better thaw them out before we go," said John. "I don't think they're supposed to be frozen."

"Yuck!" said Katie. "Don't talk about goat entrails at the dinner table!"

Dad smiled at John. "All right. One more go. But let's make sure the weather's bad. Are you sure you want bad weather for graduation?"

Chapter 55

The boys fought more than a little bit of wind as they went to school on Friday, so much so they had to lean into it. Alex stumbled when the wind suddenly let up for a brief moment. But they were in high spirits, thinking this must be a good omen for the following day.

Their day was filled with festivities, since they'd already taken their end-of-year tests. Each class held games and showed videos, and in crafts that afternoon Mr. Hume let them do anything they wanted. Alex used poster paint to create a rough drawing of Castle Alox. He held his finger to his lips when Mr. Hume said he recognized it, lest any nearby students overhear them.

"Are you going to try again?" Mr. Hume asked John while pretending to inspect a collage John was making from mail-order catalogs. "Full moon tonight."

"Tomorrow, after graduation," replied John. "The forecast is for rain and thunderstorms, so maybe it'll work this time."

Mr. Hume smiled and cocked his head sideways. "What are you making?" he asked, looking at John's project.

"It's the three of us on a flying broomstick," said John. "See, here's the twigs and here's the pole, and this is us."

"Interesting," said Mr. Hume enigmatically. "You boys be careful with lightning. Don't go on top of the tower if there's lightning nearby. Not safe."

Chapter 56

John, Conan and Alex had been looking forward to graduation for a long time, but it didn't seem quite what they expected it to be. Somehow, they thought they'd feel older, but when it happened they didn't feel any different. The boys lined up with the rest of their class, listened to boring speeches which none of them could report on later, and then walked up one by one to pick up their fake diploma—actually instructions for the parents to follow on how to get the real diploma—all rolled up with a blue ribbon around it. But first they had to shake the head teacher's hand. Cameras flashed as various students went by, and all the students cheered for their buddies. It took a very long time to go through the line.

The luncheon had originally been planned to be outdoors on the athletic field, but because of the inclement weather everyone crowded into the gymnasium, which was not very big. Conan was glum.

"Mum's not here," he confided to John and Alex. "She just started a new job and has to work weekends and can't take time off. And my father, well...."

"I got some pictures," said Dad. "We can show them to your mum."

Conan forced a smile. "You'd think he'd come for this," he said in a very small voice.

Chapter 57

On the way out of the building, they met Mr. Hume, whom they followed down into the now-familiar forbidden basement in Old Hall to retrieve the broom from its hiding place behind the big furnace.

"You won't be able to keep it down here anymore," reminded Mr. Hume. "Have you seen Marco anymore?"

"I thought I saw him about two weeks ago," said Conan. "But only out of the corner of my eye. I might've been mistaken. He was down by the bus stop."

Mr. Hume looked thoughtful as he handed the broom to John. "I don't like this Marco guy. So the police don't have any leads?"

"I don't think they're looking very hard," said Alex.

"What are you going to do with all your machines?" asked Conan, looking at the band saw, table saw, and lathe.

"I'm still negotiating with the Council. I thought I might like to take them with me to Whetherby High." Mr. Hume ran his hand over the table saw's table. "I had a hard time getting the school to buy these. Took me five years to get them all. I'd hate to leave them behind. But your parents are waiting, boys. Better not hold them up!"

The boys clambered up the stairs into the Old Hall lobby. Mr. Hume carefully locked the basement door behind him.

"So this is what you've been working on all year!" said Alex's mum.

"It's going to fly! Tonight!" exclaimed Alex.

"Now, now, dear. You mustn't get your hopes up too much."

"Keep an eye out for Marco," whispered John to Conan.

Since there was no point in driving down to the school that morning, given it was so close and parking was a problem anyway, the group walked home. Dad held a big umbrella under which he huddled with Mum. Katie and Miriam shared an umbrella, as did John and Conan. Alex walked next to his mum under her big umbrella. John held the broom so the twigs were under the umbrella, letting Conan hold the umbrella itself.

"Whoa!" said Conan, suddenly stopping.

"What is it?" hissed John.

"Not sure. Just caught a glimpse. Hold the broom so he can't see, just in case it's him."

"Where is he?"

"Usual place. Bus stop across from the Clap Hammer," said Conan, pointing.

John peered through the rain. "Let's keep walking. He won't do anything with all of us around."

Chapter 58

Saturday at four o'clock, John wrenched open the front door in response to Conan's and Alex's frantic poundings. The two rushed in, dumping their bags on the floor.

"Whew! I think I got soaked!" said Alex, taking off his coat and dumping it on the floor next to his bag.

"Got everything?" said Dad. "We'd better get going. Traffic's going to move slowly with this bad weather."

So Alex put his coat back on and the boys ran for the car. Dad helped John put the broom in, stretching from front to back, then ran into the house for the ice chest. The boys threw their bags into the trunk and scrambled to get into the car.

"The broom got wet," complained John.

"It's going to get very wet tonight," said Dad consolingly, "when you put it out on the tower."

They backed out of the Cunningham's driveway and drove down Brixton Street to the High Street. Traffic was heavy and moving at a crawl; they had to wait several minutes before being able to turn left.

"Now Miriam's the only one going to Allerton," mused Dad as they crept along, by now even with the Clap Hammer Pub.

"Marco alert!" cried Conan. "Over there! In the Clap Hammer doorway!"

John's, Dad's and Alex's heads swiveled automatically. Sure enough, it was unmistakably Marco.

"Dad! Move faster! We don't want him to see us with the broom. He'll know what we're doing!"

But Marco looked right at them. John could tell he was peering into the car. Suddenly, with a look of panic, he fled down the street with his coat flying, splashing in the puddles.

The traffic was as bad as Dad predicted; they did not arrive at the Holywell Inn until past seven o'clock. Dad spent much of the drive complaining about traffic and the other drivers, so John didn't think he was entirely supportive of their endeavor. John wanted to bring the broom into the Inn so they could keep a close eye on it while they had dinner, but Dad thought it might attract attention. What Dad really wanted to do was have some dinner and relax after the long drive. John peered out the Inn window during dinner, trying to make out shapes in the driving rainstorm. Once in a while he thought he saw a distant lightning flash out over the Irish Sea, but he couldn't be sure, since there were many lights inside the pub and it was dark and gray outside.

"Dad," whispered John urgently. "Someone just drove up and is looking inside our car!"

"Is it Marco?" asked Conan, leaning over John to have a good look out the window.

"Can't tell. He's pulled his hood over his head," replied John. He wiped the glass with his hand because his breath was causing a misty fog on the glass. "He went down the street into the tea shop."

"Let me take a look," said Dad. He slipped out of the booth and walked to the door and peered out into the driving rain. For a moment he went out the door; John could just make out Dad's outline as he double-checked that the car was locked. Dad came back in a moment later to report the broom was still inside, though it was pretty visible through the back window.

"Maybe we should bring it inside," said Alex, stirring his half-eaten soup. "But then everyone will ask questions."

Just then the same lady they'd met last time came over to check on them. "How are you, boys? Not going out again, are you? In this weather!"

John said nothing, not sure how to respond. Dad cleared his throat self-consciously. "Uh, we're fine," he said noncommittally. "The boys think this is a grand adventure."

"Well, I don't think you should be out and about! I mean, last month you were here and the weather was fine. And now why would anyone want to climb through an old castle in a driving rainstorm?" She looked pointedly at John.

"Uh," stammered John. "Has that old man been back?"

"Nope! Haven't seen hide nor hair of him. So you're going out tonight! I think you're nuts. And you won't tell me why, will you." She leaned across the table to whisper conspiratorially. "They say that old castle is magic, you know."

"Who says?" asked Conan, nonplussed. He put down his fork, which he'd just used to spear a piece of chicken.

"Local folks," she said. "Some of the old timers. They swear they've seen ghosts there. And sometimes there's a spooky feeling, you know, like something's going on you can't see."

"What do you think?" asked Alex eagerly.

"Load of old tosh, I say," she said unconvincingly, standing up and taking Dad's empty plate. "But there have been other people come here to see that castle. Always at the full moon. About five years ago there was an old couple. They said they were brother and sister, but they looked married to me, you know. In fact, come to think of it…." She trailed off.

"What?" asked Alex eagerly.

"I wonder if that old man you keep asking about is the same bloke." She stared into the distance. "Anyway, they stayed for a couple days. Always going out to the castle. And they went out at night, just like you boys are planning. Will you all be wanting any dessert? We've got some nice bread pudding."

She stood expectantly, as though waiting for Alex, Conan, and John to finish their dinners on the spot. Dad nodded, so Conan and Alex asked for dessert, but John's stomach didn't feel good. In fact, it was churning a little bit, partly because of their upcoming mission and partly because he was worried that Marco might be about. He ended up helping himself to a bit of Alex's, just so he could say he'd tasted it, because Alex said it was very good.

Once again, they had Room 3. It overlooked not only the sea but the parking lot. John perched himself by the window to keep an eye on the car, which at this point was only lit by the pub's porch light and a dim, orange streetlight. He could see the rain coming down in waves, but no one approached the car. The other car was still parked in front of the pub, the one he'd seen earlier. Why had its occupant parked in front of the pub and then entered the tea shop across the street when there was plenty of parking in front of the tea shop?

John brooded on this and the upcoming visit to the castle while the TV continued to drone on. Dad was particularly interested in the weather report, which forecast rain continuing into the next day, locally heavy.

At nine o'clock the boys put their jackets back on and trooped down the stairs. They put their hoods over their heads and waited for Dad to jump into the old Jaguar and unlock the doors before they ran through the storm and jumped into the car. The broomstick looked fine.

They drove slowly because it was hard to see. Dad had the windshield wipers going at the maximum rate and the rain beat on the roof of the car. They slowed to a crawl a couple times to check out turnoffs before they found the right one. Finally, Dad turned into the small car park and pulled to a halt in front of the path going down to the old castle, which they could just make out in the dim glow of the headlights. Just as they arrived there was a brilliant flash of lightning and a nearly instantaneous thunderclap which made them all jump.

"Did that hit the tower?" asked Alex. "Maybe we're too late!"

"I think we'd better stay in the car for a little bit," said Dad. And he wouldn't hear any objections, insisting they stay put where it was warm and dry until the lightning had moved out of the immediate area. About ten minutes later he said that it might be okay if they hurried.

By this time the car windows were completely fogged up. John made sure he had the torch. He pulled his hood over his head and cracked the door. The rain entered instantly and John felt it on his face. He jumped out and splashed in a puddle. He reached back inside to grab the broomstick. Alex and Conan jumped out, hopping up and down expectantly by the trunk. Dad made sure he had his keys. He opened the boot. Alex didn't wait to be told and opened the ice chest to pull out the plastic bag that held the goat entrails, now nearly defrosted but still cold from being on ice. Conan grabbed the bag with the snake.

Dad jumped back into the driver's seat and closed the car door, but left the headlights on with the motor idling so the boys could see down the path. John, Conan and Alex ran as fast as they dared down the uneven path, their feet splashing in puddles. John could feel the icy water leaking into his trainers. His hands were getting cold holding the broom and the flashlight. His hood slipped off at one point, but since both his hands were full, he

141

couldn't do much about it until they had reached the safety of the tower. The boys ran inside and paused to catch their breath.

"Whew!" said Alex.

"Be careful going up the stairs," cautioned John. This was a good idea since water was cascading down the stairs from the opening that led to the roof.

"Let me take the torch," suggested Conan. "All I've got is the snake."

So they trooped up the stairs, staying close to the outer wall because they didn't trust the rickety handrail. Soon they were atop the tower, once again in the rain. John quickly put down the broomstick. Alex hastily plopped the bag of entrails atop the broom and Conan put the plastic bag with the snake in it atop the broom also, stooping down to make sure the snake was draped across the broomstick.

A bright lightning strike hit the beach nearby, accompanied by an instantaneous and almighty CRACK that reverberated for several seconds. Alex was so surprised he fell over.

"Don't fall through the hole!" shouted Conan, grabbing Alex and pulling him away.

"Let's get out of here!" shouted John.

Alex went down first, followed by Conan and then John. They regrouped inside the tower at the base of the stairs.

"We'd better make a run for the car," urged Conan.

As the wind screamed the boys clambered over the remains of the wall and ran pellmell toward the car park. The old Jaguar's headlights lit up the raindrops as they splashed forward. But just then another car turned into the parking area, its headlights sweeping across the castle walls. It drove straight toward them. The driver was too eager and did not stop short of the rocks marking the edge of the parking area. The headlights flew upward as the car rolled onto the rocks. As soon as the car stopped, a lone figure jumped out and ran toward them, silhouetted in the headlights.

"Marco!" exclaimed Conan.

"What do we do?" shouted Alex.

"Make for the car," urged John.

With earth-shattering thunder, lightning struck just behind the cars. In the brilliant flash, John saw that Dad had jumped out of the old Jaguar. The thunderclap was so loud the boys hit the mud in fright.

"Back in the castle!" shouted John. "We've got to wait until it's safe."

They stumbled backward, their night vision still overwhelmed by the brilliance of the lightning bolt.

"What'll we do about Marco?" shouted Alex.

"Wait, I dropped the torch," yelled Conan. He stooped to pick it up.

"Conan, come on! Alex!" shouted John as he reached the castle.

They clambered over the rocks and were soon in the tower. John and Conan scrambled to look out one of the archer's windows at the parking lot. Alex wasn't tall enough and tried to climb up. In the light of another lightning bolt, they saw Dad struggling with Marco.

"What's happening?" yelled Alex.

Another lightning bolt, this one further away, showed one man lying on his back and the other on his knees. John and Conan couldn't tell who was who.

"Maybe your dad knocked him out," suggested Conan.

"Can't tell from here," replied John. "Let's go look."

But as the boys climbed out of the tower once more, they heard the voice they least wanted to hear.

"You can't hide from me any longer," yelled Marco above the wind.

Conan aimed the torch in the direction of the voice. Marco, blood on his face, was only feet from the castle wall.

"Conan, pick up a stone. Throw it at him!"

"I can't! All the old stones are too big."

"Up the stairs!" commanded John.

"What good's that going to do?" asked Alex, who nevertheless ran up the steps.

John and Conan quickly followed.

"You can't escape, you filth!" yelled Marco. "I'm coming up after you. I'll have that book yet!"

143

"We don't have the book," yelled Alex.

"You must! That's why you're here!" exclaimed Marco.

Conan directed the torch downward. Marco was cautiously climbing the wet stairs. Alex jumped for the broom and pulled off the bag of defrosted entrails. He hurried over to the other edge of the opening. Without waiting, he dropped the bag onto Marco. Marco fell backward, screaming obscenities. Conan jumped to the broom, grabbed the snake, and threw it at Marco, but he was once again ascending the stairs.

"What do we do now?" yelled Alex.

"Look!" replied John. "Dad's up!"

Sure enough, outlined against the Jaguar's headlights was Dad, walking lopsidedly toward the tower.

"Conan, Alex, quick—the broom!" yelled John.

"Are we going to throw it at him?" begged Conan. "Not after all the work we've done!"

"No! Get on! Now!"

John jumped so the broom was beneath his feet. Conan jumped behind him, and Alex behind him. John grabbed the broomstick and found it weightless. He pulled it up underneath them.

"Will it work?" demanded Alex. "Marco's coming."

"Did lightning strike the tower?" yelled Conan. "Hurry!"

"Hold on!" yelled John.

He pulled up on the broomstick. The boys all whooped as their feet left the ground. It had worked!

The broom seemed to obey John's thoughts. He swiveled.

Marco jumped up onto the tower and lunged for the boys.

"He's got my foot!" screamed Alex in panic.

"Hold on!" repeated John.

He lifted up more, now caught in the strong sea breeze. Alex screamed some more. But suddenly the extra weight was gone and the broom shot into the air with the three boys aboard.

"My shoe," mumbled Alex. "I don't have another pair of shoes."

John aimed the broom at Dad and soon they were along side him, drenched in the driving rain.

"Dad, go back to the hotel. We'll distract Marco and then follow you."

As he spoke, Marco lunged down the path and grabbed at the boys. John pulled the broom higher. Marco rounded on Dad.

"You did this! You let them! I'll have that book yet!"

He swung at Dad, who blocked the punch. John brought the broom down and kicked Marco's head. Marco went down, howling.

"Dad! Go!" screamed John. "Just go!"

Marco ran after Dad but John hit him again. Marco turned and jumped at the boys. In response, John backed up a few feet, hovering only inches in the air. Just as John had hoped, Marco lunged for them. John kept backing up.

Outlined in the headlights, Dad stood as the boys backed away. After several seconds, he turned and ran toward the car. In moments the headlights swung around as he headed east toward the hotel.

John pulled up into the rain until they could barely see the castle's outline below them, still lit by Marco's headlights. Marco peered up into the rain, then ran back to his car and came back moments later with a powerful torch. This he used to sweep the skies.

"Over the sea," urged Conan. "He won't look for us there."

"Just don't drop too much," squeaked Alex. "I don't want to drown."

The boys stayed as far away from the castle as they dared. They watched Marco walk all the way around the castle ruins. He ran up the stairs, shined his torch around, then went back down the stairs and crawled out of the tower. Slowly, he walked back to his car, occasionally turning to search the sky. He shook his fists in the air, but the boys couldn't hear what he said over the noise of the wind.

"My shoe!" urged Alex. "Now that he's leaving, can I please get my shoe back?"

John swooped down to the top of the tower, but before he could touch down Marco turned around and ran to the tower. Cautiously, John backed off. The boys watched Marco jump up the stairs. He looked around for a moment, then grabbed Alex's shoe and the torch Conan had been using. He pocketed the torch, but held up the shoe. He was pointed away from the boys, but from this close they could hear him clearly.

"This is all I need," he shouted. "I have you now." He jumped down the stairs and ran back to his car. The boys approached to watch. Marco gunned the engine and threw the car into reverse, but the rear wheels just spun. Marco tried driving forward, with the same results. His car was pinned on the rocks.

"John," urged Conan. "Let's go back to the hotel. Marco can't do anything to us now."

"What does he want with my shoe?" whined Alex.

"I don't know," replied John. "Hold on. We have to follow the road back to the hotel. Watch out for wires."

"I'm freezing," said Conan. "Hurry."

Chapter 59

The rain still fell hard as the boys approached the hotel. Dad was outside, pacing back and forth by the car. John angled the broom so it was above the hotel's porch light.

"We're up here!" yelled John.

Dad peered up into the rain.

"We're going to set down over there," said John, pointing, "where it's dark."

Dad ran to the dark corner of the parking lot as John brought the broom down. As soon as the boys were off, Dad grabbed all three in a bear hug.

"It worked!" exclaimed Dad, but quietly so people in the hotel wouldn't wake up. "I don't believe it."

"Marco's stuck at the castle," reported Conan. "His car's hung up on a rock."

"He's got my shoe," muttered Alex.

"And the torch," said Conan.

"Dad, Marco will come back. We should go home," said John.

"It worked! I don't believe it!" replied Dad, shaking his head and staring at the broomstick.

"Mr Cunningham, of course it worked," admonished Alex. "It's magic, right?"

"Wow!" said Dad. "But we'd better get you inside and dried off. Let's go."

The three sodden, shivering boys followed. John held the broomstick. Dad used his room key to open the hotel's front door and ushered the boys inside.

Standing inside was the landlady. She blocked the hall and stared at the boys and the broomstick. Dad hovered in the background. John was afraid and tried to hide the broomstick behind him, but she had a wide smile.

"I had my suspicions," she said, leaning toward them. "And here you are. Such young boys...you must be something special. So Miriam gave you the book, did she? Yes, I can tell from your faces. Well, good for you! Now you be safe on that thing, do you hear? And I've left extra towels in your room and turned up the water heater for the showers. Best get upstairs!"

The boys clambered up the stairs.

"How does she know the old woman's name?" asked Conan.

"Maybe there are lots of magical people we don't know," mused Alex.

"I suspect we'll be meeting some of them soon," said John. "Right now I want to be in a hot shower!"

"Then let's do that," said Dad.

And so that's what they did. They grinned and jumped, making their way to the floor's community shower room. The piping hot water pushed their fears away. In their jubilant mood, they chattered happily about what they'd do with their new flying broomstick.

- 3 0 -

Book 2, *Saving Conan*, is the next in the *Three on a Broomstick* series. Conan falls into an ancient trap in the ruins of a secret, magical castle. John and Alex have to save him before the big storm floods the place. And Marco remains as determined as ever to have the book.

Keep up to date with the great adventures in the *Three on a Broomstick* series by visiting

www.ThreeOnABroomstick.com

www.MtSneffelsPress.com

See David Casler's author page on Amazon at

www.amazon.com/-/e/B00471I0Q4